Faust

Ivan Turgenev

Translated by Hugh Aplin

ALMA CLASSICS

ALMA CLASSICS LTD
London House
243-253 Lower Mortlake Road
Richmond
Surrey TW9 2LL
United Kingdom
www.almaclassics.com

Faust first published in 1855
Yakov Pasynkov first published in 1855
This translation first published by Hesperus Press in 2003
This new revised edition first pulbished by Alma Classics Ltd in 2012

Printed in Great Britain by CPI Antony Rowe

Typesetting and eBook design by Tetragon

ISBN: 978-1-84749-218-0

Contents

Ivan Turgenev (1818–83)

Pauline Viardot

Louis Viardot

"Paulinette",
Turgenev's daughter

Marya Savina as Verochka in
A Month in the Country

Bougival, France, where Turgenev spent the end of his life

Turgenev's funeral procession in Petersburg in 1883

Drawing of Ivan Turgenev
by Adolph Menzel

Introduction

More than any other of the great Russian writers of the nineteenth century, Ivan Turgenev was, by instinct and experience, a European. He spent the major part of his adult life abroad, and a list of his literary friends reads like the roll-call for a masterclass in prose-writing of the age of Realism – Henry James, Gustave Flaubert, Émile Zola, Guy de Maupassant, to name but a few. As a member of the Russian nobility, he was reared on a rich European cultural diet; and he was, broadly speaking, sympathetic to the Westernizers in their great debate with the Slavophiles about Russia's position vis-à-vis Western Europe, a debate that was central to much of Russia's cultural history during his lifetime. It should therefore come as no surprise that Turgenev included many a reference to Western art, philosophy and literature in his writings. What may be surprising is that no major German names can be found to figure among the sample of friends listed above; this is, however, a matter of mere historical chance, for, as the title of this volume suggests, German literature was just as important for Turgenev as were, say, French and English. Indeed, if allusions, quotations and reminiscences are totted up, then it is Germany's greatest poet, Johann Wolfgang von Goethe, who proves to figure in Turgenev's wide range of reference more frequently than any other foreign writer. Not for nothing did the Russian label himself "an inveterate Goethe man".

Turgenev's enthusiasm for things German can be traced back to his youth, when he spent the years from 1838 to 1841 studying at Berlin University. The city at that time was something of a philosophical and cultural Mecca for young Russians, and it was there that the still rather immature future writer made the acquaintance of many an older luminary. Among them were the Moscow University history professor Timofei Granovsky, Nikolai Stankevich, the immensely influential hub of a philosophical circle, who died of consumption in 1840 at the age of only twenty-seven, and the anarchist-to-be Mikhail Bakunin. While men such as these played important roles in Turgenev's general development, his specific fascination with German culture and, first and foremost, with Goethe would have been fired by meetings with the great man's one-time close friend, Bettina von Arnim, and his future English biographer, G.H. Lewes. Certainly, by the time he settled back in Russia Turgenev was said to know the first part of his favourite work, Goethe's *Faust*, all but by heart, rather like the narrator of his own story of the same name.

His desire to propagate Goethe in Russia is attested to by his translations of various parts of the German's literary output, including the final scene from Part One of *Faust*, which he published in 1844. That same year a translation by Mikhail Vronchenko of the whole of Part One of *Faust* appeared in St Petersburg, prompting Turgenev to write a lengthy review. Not only did it deal with the merits of Vronchenko's labour, it also summarized Turgenev's own opinions of Goethe and *Faust* as they stood at that time. These were not what they might have been but a year or two earlier, for under the influence of Vissarion Belinsky, the leading Russian critic of the day, Turgenev was now disapproving of the egotism, individualism and romanticism he perceived as central to Goethe's tragedy. Nonetheless, he still regarded it as "the fullest expression of the age when battle was finally joined between the old days and the new, and men acknowledged that nothing was unshakeable except for human reason and Nature". In particular, he valued highly the aspiration it embodied to be free of "the yoke of tradition, scholasticism and any sort of authority in general"; Goethe, he wrote, "was the first to stand up for the rights of the individual, passionate, limited man".

Such, then, was the background against which Turgenev's story *Faust* was written just over a decade after the publication of this review. And although *Yakov Pasynkov*, the second story in this volume, may not have the same self-evident links with German culture as Turgenev's *Faust*, still much of its substance can be seen to stem ultimately from similar sources.

Turgenev wrote *Faust* between June and August 1856, for the most part while living at Spasskoye, his late mother's estate in Oryol Province. The descriptions of the estate in the story closely resemble the reality of Spasskoye, the narrator's past is very similar to Turgenev's own, and there may have been a further autobiographical strand in the plot of *Faust* too. For it was in 1854 that Turgenev first met his neighbour, Maria Tolstaya, the sister of Leo Tolstoy, at her nearby home, Pokrovskoye. She was already married, but such niceties never prevented Turgenev from forming attachments, as is amply demonstrated by his lifelong relationship with Pauline Viardot. The physical description of Vera, the heroine of *Faust*, is reminiscent of Maria, and the idea of Vera's ignorance of creative literature may have been suggested by Maria's indifference to poetry. It is certainly tempting to picture Turgenev charting his own feelings for his charming neighbour through the relations between his fictional characters, even though the denouements in life and fiction were to differ very markedly.

The key event in the plot of Turgenev's *Faust* is the narrator's reading of Goethe's *Faust* to the heroine. Such literary communication was a regular motif in Turgenev's works in the 1850s; the reading of one of Alexander Pushkin's poems in *A Quiet Spot* (1854) leads to catastrophe; in *Rudin* (1856) the eponymous hero reads several works of German literature, including *Faust*, to the young Russian girl who loves him; and in *Asya* (1857) the narrator's declaiming of Goethe's *Hermann and Dorothea* has a remarkable impact upon the enigmatic heroine. Less characteristic of Turgenev at this time, albeit not later on in his career, is the intrusion of a supernatural element in the development of the plot. This led to a degree of criticism from those of his contemporaries who insisted on the pre-eminence of realism in literature; but such disapproval might be countered with the argument that the supernatural should be interpreted here not literally, but psychologically, as the projection of the characters' troubled feelings about their situation.

In any event, the nature of the relationship between hero and heroine, the sense of guilt and resignation that pervades the story's conclusion, the self-centred, introspective character of the male protagonist – all these are elements immediately recognizable to those familiar with Turgenev's oeuvre as a whole. And these features are discernible to one degree or another in *Yakov Pasynkov* too.

Turgenev wrote this story in an even shorter time than *Faust*, in less than two weeks in February 1855, although he did make some significant changes between its first publication in a journal later that year and its subsequent reissue in book form. The most obvious of these was the exclusion of the story's epigraph, which had immediately forged a link with German culture, for it was a quotation from Friedrich von Schiller – "Dare to err and to dream".

Work on *Yakov Pasynkov* was simultaneous with that on *Rudin*, and the interrelatedness of Turgenev's writings in the mid-1850s is suggested by the removal of the original opening of the former story to the latter, and by the transfer of the name Pasynkov (derived from the Russian word for "stepson" or, figuratively, "outcast") in the opposite direction. And just as Turgenev drew on his own life as a student in Germany for the background of the narrator of *Faust*, so he used aspects of his own pre-Berlin life for the early biography of his narrator in

Yakov Pasynkov. But a strong link with Germany is established in this story too through the figure of Yakov Pasynkov himself. Most obviously, he is a great admirer of German art, reading Schiller in the original and revering the music of Schubert. He is, indeed, in general a representative of the generation of young Russians who grew up under the influence of German idealism in the 1830s. Critics have identified the youthful Belinsky, before his move away from idealism, as the specific prototype for the character of Pasynkov; yet it might also be suggested that those Russians Turgenev knew in Berlin, such as Stankevich, already long dead, and Granovsky, who died in 1855, joined Belinsky (who had died in 1848) in Turgenev's consciousness to form a composite portrait of a doomed but memorable romantic. Certainly the relationship between the story's narrator and its hero, Pasynkov, could be seen to echo that between Turgenev and any one of these mentors.

But irrespective of its model, it is Pasynkov's very nature, with its burning sincerity, its enthusiasm, kindness and generosity, and its thirst for truth and beauty, that is of supreme importance. It was the contrast between such a figure and the self-obsessed self-analysts whose introspection leads to spiritual paralysis, pessimistic scepticism, and misanthropy that Turgenev was to explore in his lecture '*Hamlet* and *Don Quixote*' (1860). The conclusion he reached was that the actual achievement of a man is arguably of less significance than the nature of his aspirations and the manner of his life. This was a lesson that Turgenev had been taught by Granovsky in Berlin in the 1830s, and it was a belief held by Goethe too.

Turgenev is perhaps best known for his depiction of "superfluous men", Russian Hamlets incapable of fulfilling their potential, and although he proved his own worth as one of the finest of all Russian novelists, he was himself close to this type in temperament. Yet his writings also include numerous examples of the optimistic, active idealist, the quixotic character whose origins, for him, are to be traced no less to Germany than to Spain. The two stories in this volume reflect admirably the debt that Turgenev owed to German culture, while at the same time underlining his right to a place of honour not only on a Russian Parnassus, but on a European one too.

– Hugh Aplin

Faust

A Story in Nine Letters

*Entbehren sollst du, sollst entbehren.**

FIRST LETTER

From Pavel Alexandrovich B——
to Semyon Nikolayevich V——

The village of M——oye, 6th June 1850

I arrived here three days ago, my dear friend, and, as promised, am taking up my pen and writing to you. There has been a sprinkling of light rain since morning: it's not possible to go out and, what's more, I feel like having a little chat with you. Here I am again in my old nest, where I haven't been – it's frightening to say it – for nine whole years. If you think about it, it really is as if I've become a different person. And I am, indeed, different: do you remember, in the drawing room, my great-grandmother's dingy little mirror with those strange little scrolls in the corners? You were always wondering what it had seen a hundred years ago. As soon as I arrived I went up to it – and became embarrassed in spite of myself. I suddenly saw how I've aged and changed of late. But then I'm not the only one that's aged. My little house, which has long been ramshackle, is now scarcely standing, it's grown crooked and sunk into the ground. My kind Vasilyevna, the housekeeper (you've not forgotten her, I'm sure: she fed you such marvellous jam), has become quite shrivelled and bent; when she saw me, she was unable to cry out and didn't burst into tears, but just started groaning, had a coughing fit, sat down on a chair in exhaustion, and waved her hand. The old man, Terenty, is still in good form, stands up as straight as ever and twists his legs about as he walks, wearing the same funny yellow nankeen trousers and the same squeaky goatskin shoes with the high instep and bows that you many a time found touching... But my God! How those trousers flap about now on his skinny legs! How white his hair has become! And his face has quite shrivelled up to the size of a small fist; and when he started to talk to me, when he began to make arrangements and give out orders in the next room, I found it funny, and yet felt sorry for him too. He's lost all his teeth, and he speaks in a mumble accompanied by a whistling and a hissing. The garden, on the other hand, has become amazingly pretty: the modest little lilac, acacia and honeysuckle bushes (you remember, it was you and I that planted them) have filled out into magnificent dense shrubs; the birches and maples – they've all shot up and spread wide; the lime-tree walks have become particularly attractive. I love those walks, I love the delicate grey-green colour and the subtle scent of the air beneath their vaults; I love the dappled network of bright little circles across the dark earth – as you know, I have no sand. My favourite oak sapling has already become a young oak tree. In the middle of the day yesterday I sat for more than an hour in its shade on a bench. I felt very happy. The grass was flourishing so cheerfully all around; a golden light, strong and soft, lay on everything; it even penetrated into the shade... and the birds that could be heard! I hope you haven't forgotten that birds are my passion. Turtle doves cooed incessantly, every now and then an oriole would whistle, a chaffinch did its sweet little thing, the thrushes got angry and twittered away, a cuckoo responded in the distance; suddenly, like a maniac, a woodpecker would utter its piercing cry. I listened, listened to all this soft, commingled babbling, and did not want to stir, and it was hard to tell if it was idleness or emotion in my heart. And it's not just the garden that has grown: my eye is constantly being caught by solid, hefty lads, in whom I simply cannot recognize the little boys I knew before. And your favourite, little Timosha, has now become such a grown-up Timofei, you just can't imagine.

You were afraid for his health then and predicted he'd be consumptive; but if you looked now at his huge red hands, the way they poke out of the tight sleeves of his nankeen frock coat, and what rounded, thick muscles he has bulging out everywhere! The back of his neck is like a bull's, and his head is covered in tight blond curls – a perfect Farnese Hercules!* But then his face has changed less than those of the others, it hasn't even grown much in size, and his cheerful – yawning, as you used to say – smile has remained the same. I've taken him on as my valet; I got rid of the one from St Petersburg while in Moscow: he was so very fond of putting me to shame and making me feel his superiority as regards the ways of the capital. I didn't find a single one of my dogs; they've all died off. Only Nefka lived longer than all the rest, but even she didn't stay waiting long enough, the way Argos did for Ulysses; she was not fated to see her former master and hunting companion with her dimmed eyes. But Shavka is alive, and barks in the same hoarse way, and has one ear torn in the same way, and there are burrs in her tail, as there should be. I've moved into your former little room. The sun beats into it, it's true, and there are lots of flies in it; on the other hand there is less of the smell of an old house than in all the other rooms. It's a strange thing! That musty, slightly sour and faded smell has a powerful effect on my imagination: I can't say that I find it unpleasant, on the contrary; but it makes me sad and, in the end, depressed. Just like you, I am very fond of old, bow-fronted chests with brass finger-plates, white armchairs with oval backs and crooked legs, fly-blown glass chandeliers with a large egg-shaped piece of lilac foil in the middle – in short, all sorts of furniture from our grandfathers' time; but I can't bear seeing it all continually: a sort of uneasy dreariness (that's it precisely!) will take hold of me. The furniture in the room I've moved into is the most ordinary home-made stuff; however, I've left a long, narrow chest of drawers in the corner, on which various pieces of antiquated green and blue blown glassware can scarcely be seen through the dust; and I've ordered to be hung on the wall, do you remember, that portrait of a woman that you called the portrait of Manon Lescaut.* It's become a little darker over these nine years, but the eyes look out just as pensively, slyly and tenderly, the lips laugh just as frivolously and sadly, and the rose with half its petals pulled off droops just as gently from her slender fingers. I'm most amused by the curtains in my room. They were once green, but have turned yellow in the sun: painted across them in black dye are scenes from d'Arlincourt's *The Hermit*.* On one curtain this hermit, with the most enormous beard and bulging eyes and wearing sandals, is enticing some dishevelled young lady away into the mountains; on the other there is a violent struggle taking place between four knights wearing berets and with padded shoulders; one is lying dead *en raccourci*;* in short, every horror is represented, while all around there is such untroubled calm, and the curtains themselves reflect the light onto the ceiling so meekly... A sort of spiritual hush has come upon me since I moved in here; I don't want to do anything, I don't want to see anyone, there's nothing to dream about, I'm too idle to have any serious thoughts – but I'm not too idle to think: these are two different things, as you know very well yourself. Memories of childhood crowded in on me at first... wherever I went, whatever I looked at, they rose up from all sides, clear, clear to the tiniest details, and seemingly fixed in their sharp definition... Then these memories were replaced by others, then... then I gradually turned away from the past, and there remained only a sort of drowsy weight in my breast. Imagine! Sitting on a weir underneath a willow tree, all of a sudden I unexpectedly burst out crying, and would have cried for a long time, despite my already advanced years, had I not been put to shame by a passing peasant woman, who gave me a curious look and then, without turning her face towards me, bowed straight and low and went on by. I should very much like to remain in a mood like this (it goes without saying that I won't be crying any more) right up until the time I leave here, until September, that is, and I should be most upset if any of the neighbours took it into their heads to call on me. But there seems to be no reason to fear that; I don't even have any near neighbours. I'm sure you'll understand me; you know from your own experience how beneficial solitude can often be... I need it now, after my various wanderings.

But I shan't be bored. I brought several books with me, and I have a respectable library here. Yesterday I opened up all the cabinets and spent a long time rummaging among the mouldering books. I found many curious things that I had not noticed before: *Candide* in a manuscript translation from the 1770s; newspapers and journals from the same time; *The Triumphant Chameleon* (Mirabeau, that is); *Le Paysan perverti*, etc.* I came across children's books, both my own and those of my father and grandmother, and even, imagine, my great-grandmother: one dreadfully tatty French grammar in a mottled binding has written on it in large letters: *Ce livre appartient à m-lle Eudoxie de Lavrine*,* and the year is marked down as 1741. I saw the books that I once brought from abroad, among them Goethe's *Faust*. Perhaps you're not aware that there was a time when I knew *Faust* off by heart (the first part, it goes without saying), word for word; I couldn't read it enough... But new days, new ways, and in the course of the last nine years I've scarcely had occasion to pick Goethe up. With what an inexpressible feeling did I catch sight of the little book I knew all too well (a poor edition from 1828)! I carried it off with me, lay down on the bed, and began to read. What an effect the entire magnificent first scene had on me! The appearance of the Earth Spirit, his words, you remember, "On the waves of life, in the whirlwind of creation", aroused in me a tremor long untasted and a chill of rapture. I remembered everything: Berlin, my time as a student, Fräulein Clara Stich, and Seydelmann in the role of Mephistopheles, and Radziwill's music, and absolutely everything...* I couldn't get to sleep for a long time: my youth came and stood before me like a ghost; like fire, like poison it ran through my veins, my heart swelled and didn't want to contract, something tugged at its strings, and desires began to seethe...

Those are the dreams that your friend of almost forty fell into, sitting all alone in his lonely little house! What if someone had spied on me? Well, so what? I wouldn't have been ashamed at all. Being ashamed is a sign of youth as well; and do you know why I've begun to notice that I'm getting old? Here's why. I try now to exaggerate to myself my cheerful feelings and curb my sad ones, whereas in the days of my youth I did quite the reverse. You'd fuss over your sadness like a treasure, and be shamefaced about a burst of gaiety...

Yet it seems to me, nevertheless, that regardless of all my experience of life, there is still something on this earth, my friend Horatio,* that I haven't tried, and that that "something" is all but the most important thing.

Oh dear, what have I ended up writing! Goodbye! Until the next time. What are you doing in St Petersburg? Incidentally, Savyely, my cook here in the country, asks to be remembered to you. He's aged as well, but not too much, he's grown rather fat and flabby. He's just as good at making chicken soup with boiled onions, curd tarts with decorative edging, and sour cucumber skilly, that renowned dish of the steppes, skilly, that made your tongue turn white and go stiff for a whole day. But on the other hand, his roast meat turns out just as dry as ever, so dry you can knock it about on your plate, but it's still just like cardboard. Anyway, goodbye!

Your P.B.

SECOND LETTER

From the same to the same

The village of M——oye, 12th June 1850

I have quite an important piece of news to tell you, dear friend. Listen! Yesterday, before lunch, I felt like taking a walk, only not in the garden; I set off along the road to town. Striding quickly down a long straight road without any objective is very pleasant. It's as if you're doing something, hurrying somewhere. I look, and there's a carriage coming towards me. "It's not going to my place, is it?" I thought with secret terror… But no: in the carriage sits a gentleman I don't know with a moustache. I was reassured. But suddenly this gentleman, drawing level with me, orders the coachman to stop the horses, raises his cap courteously, and even more courteously asks me if I am not so-and-so, calling me by my name. I stop in my turn and, with the enthusiasm of a prisoner being taken for interrogation, I reply that "I am so-and-so", while staring blankly at the gentleman with the moustache and thinking to myself: "But I've seen him somewhere, haven't I!"

"Don't you recognize me?" he says, climbing down in the meantime from the carriage.

"No, sir."

"But I recognized you straight away."

It turned out little by little that it was Priyimkov, you remember, our one-time companion at university. At this moment, dear Semyon Nikolayich, you're thinking: "What kind of important piece of news is this then? Priyimkov, so far as I can recall, was a rather shallow fellow, albeit not vicious and not stupid." That's all true, my good friend, but listen to how the conversation continued.

"I was very glad," he says, "when I heard you were visiting your village, right next door to us. But I wasn't the only one who was glad."

"Might I learn," I asked, "who else could have been so kind?..."

"My wife."

"Your wife?"

"Yes, my wife: she's an old acquaintance of yours."

"Well, might I learn your wife's name?"

"Her name is Vera Nikolayevna; her maiden name was Yeltsova..."

"Vera Nikolayevna!" I involuntarily exclaim...

And it's this that is that important piece of news I was telling you about at the beginning of the letter.

But perhaps you find nothing important in this either... I shall have to tell you something from my past... my distant past.

When you and I left university together in 183–, I was twenty-three years old. You entered the civil service; I, as you are aware, resolved to set off for Berlin. But there was nothing for me to do in Berlin any earlier than October. I took a fancy to spending the summer in Russia, in the countryside, to being good and idle for the last time, before then taking up work in earnest. To what extent this last intention was realized – there's no point in enlarging on that now... "But where am I to spend the summer?" I wondered. I didn't feel like going to my own village: my father had recently died, I had no close relations, I was afraid of loneliness, boredom... And so I gladly accepted the proposal of one of my relatives, a cousin once removed, to be his guest on his estate in the province of T——. He was a well-to-do man, kind and straightforward, he lived like a lord, and had a home like a palace. I moved in with him. My cousin's family was a large one: two sons and five daughters. And in addition there were masses of people living in his house. Guests were constantly dropping in – and yet it wasn't much fun. The days flowed by noisily, there was no opportunity for privacy. Everything was done together, everyone tried to amuse themselves with something or other, to think something or other up, and by the end of the day everyone was dreadfully tired. There was something vulgar about that life. I was already beginning to dream of leaving and was only waiting for my cousin's name day to pass, but on the name day itself, at the ball, I saw Vera Nikolayevna Yeltsova – and I stayed.

She was then sixteen years old. She lived with her mother on a small estate about five versts* from my cousin. Her father – a remarkable man, they say – had rapidly attained the rank of colonel and would have gone still further, but was killed as a young man, accidentally shot by a comrade while hunting. He left Vera Nikolayevna still a child. Her mother was an extraordinary woman too: she spoke several languages, knew a great deal. She was seven or eight years older than her husband, whom she had married for love; he had carried her away in secret from her parents' home. She barely survived his loss, and right up until her death (according to Priyimkov, she died soon after her daughter's wedding) wore only black dresses. I remember her face vividly: expressive, dark, with thick hair that had turned grey, large, severe eyes, in which the light seemed to have gone out, and a narrow, straight nose. Her father – his name was Ladanov – had lived for some fifteen years in Italy. Vera Nikolayevna's mother was born of a simple peasant woman from Albano, who was killed the day after she gave birth by her fiancé, a Trasteverino,* from whom Ladanov had stolen her... This story caused a great stir in its time. Returning to Russia, Ladanov never left his study, let alone his house, and occupied himself with chemistry, anatomy, secret spells, wanting to prolong human life, imagining it was possible to commune with spirits, summon up the dead... His neighbours considered him a wizard. He was extremely fond of his daughter, taught her everything himself, but did not forgive her for running away with Yeltsov, did not let either her or her husband into his sight, foretold a life of sorrow for them both, and died alone. Having been left a widow, Mrs Yeltsova dedicated all her free time to the upbringing of her daughter, and received almost nobody. When I made Vera Nikolayevna's acquaintance, just imagine, she had not been to a single town from the day she was born, not even the one in her own district.

Vera Nikolayevna did not resemble ordinary young Russian ladies: a particular sort of imprint lay upon her. From the first I was struck by the astonishing calm in all her movements and speech. She did not seem to make a fuss about anything, did not become anxious, replied simply and intelligently, listened attentively. The expression on her face was sincere and truthful like that of a child, but somewhat cold and unchanging, albeit not pensive. She was gay but rarely, and not in the same way as others: the clarity of an innocent soul, more comforting than gaiety, shone throughout her being. She was of no great height, had a very good figure, was rather slim, had regular and gentle features, a fine, even forehead, golden-russet hair, a straight nose like her mother's, quite full lips; her darkly tinged grey eyes gazed somehow too directly from beneath fluffy, upward-curving lashes. Her hands were not large, but not very pretty: people of talent don't have such hands... and indeed, Vera Nikolayevna did not have any particular talents. Her voice rang like that of a seven-year-old girl's. At my cousin's ball I was presented to her mother, and a few days later I went to visit them for the first time.

Mrs Yeltsova was a very strange woman with a strong character, insistent and intense. She had a powerful influence on me: I was both respectful and a little afraid of her. She had everything done according to a system, and she had brought her daughter up according to a system too, but had not restricted her freedom. Her daughter loved her and had blind faith in her. Mrs Yeltsova only had to give her a book and say: "don't read this page", and she would miss out the preceding page rather than catch a glimpse of the forbidden one. Yet Mrs Yeltsova had her *idées fixes* as well, her hobby horses. For example, she feared like fire anything that might affect the imagination; and so her daughter, right up to the age of seventeen, had not read a single story, nor a single poem, whereas in geography, history and even in natural history she would quite often have me stumped – me, a graduate, and not a bad one either, as you perhaps recall. I once tried to have a talk with Mrs Yeltsova about her hobby horse, although it was difficult to draw her into conversation: she was very taciturn. She only shook her head.

"You say," she said finally, "reading works of poetry is *both* beneficial *and* pleasant... I think in life one has to choose in advance: *either* the beneficial *or* the pleasant, and so come to a decision once and for all. I too once wanted to combine both the one and the other... It is not possible, and it leads either to ruin or vulgarity."

Yes, that woman was an astonishing creature, an honest, proud creature, not without fanaticism and superstition of a sort. "I'm afraid of life," she said to me once. And she really was afraid of it, she was afraid of those secret forces on which life is built and which only occasionally, but suddenly, burst through to the surface. Woe betide the person over whom they rage! Those forces had affected Yeltsova in a terrible way: remember the deaths of her mother, her husband, her father... That would have frightened anybody. Never did I see her smile. It was as if she had locked herself up and thrown the key away. She must have suffered much grief in her time and had never shared it with anyone: she hid it all away inside her. To such a degree had she trained herself not to give free rein to her feelings that she was even ashamed of displaying her passionate love for her daughter; not once did she kiss her in my presence, never did she call her by a pet name, it was always: "Vera". I remember one remark of hers: I said to her once that we, people today, were all a little damaged... "There's no point in doing a little damage to yourself," she pronounced, "you should break yourself completely or else not touch..."

Very few people called on Yeltsova, but I visited her often. I was secretly conscious that she was well disposed towards me, and I liked Vera Nikolayevna very much. She and I talked, went for walks… Her mother did not bother us; the daughter did not herself like to be without her mother, and I, for my part, did not feel any need for any private conversation either. Vera Nikolayevna had the strange habit of thinking out loud; in the night-time she would talk in her sleep loudly and distinctly about what had struck her in the course of the day. Once, after looking at me closely, leaning her cheek gently on her hand, as was her habit, she said, "I think B. is a good man, but he can't be relied on." Relations between us were the most amicable and equable; only once did it seem to me that I had discerned somewhere there, far away, in the very depths of her bright eyes, something strange, a certain languor and tenderness… But perhaps I was mistaken.

Meanwhile the days were passing, and it was already time for me to prepare for my departure. But I continued to linger. Sometimes, when I thought, when I remembered that soon I would not be seeing this sweet girl to whom I had become so attached, I would start to feel awful… Berlin was beginning to lose its magnetic power. I did not dare to admit to myself what was happening inside me, and I did not even understand what was happening inside me – it was as if there were a mist adrift in my soul. Finally, one morning, everything suddenly became clear to me. "What more am I to seek?" I thought. "Where am I to aspire? After all, the truth is hard to come by. Wouldn't I do better to stay here and get married?" And just imagine, this idea of marriage didn't scare me at all then. On the contrary, I was glad of it. Moreover, that same day I announced my intention, only not to Vera Nikolayevna, as might have been expected, but to Yeltsova herself. The old woman looked at me.

"No, my dear," she said, "you go to Berlin, do a little more damage to yourself. You're kind; but a different sort of husband is needed for Vera."

I dropped my eyes, blushed, and at once, which will probably surprise you still more, inwardly concurred with Yeltsova. I left a week later, and since then I had never again seen either her or Vera Nikolayevna.

I've described my experiences to you in brief, because I know you don't like anything "expansive". After arriving in Berlin I very soon forgot Vera Nikolayevna... But, I confess, the unexpected news about her excited me. I was struck by the idea that she was so close, that she was my neighbour, that I would see her in a few days' time. As though from out of the ground, the past had suddenly risen up before me, had drawn really close to me. Priyimkov announced to me that he had paid me a visit with the specific aim of renewing our old acquaintance and that he hoped to see me at his house in a very short time. He informed me that he had served in the cavalry, retired as a lieutenant, bought an estate eight kilometres from me and intended to farm, that he used to have three children, but two had died, and only a five-year-old daughter remained.

"And does your wife remember me?" I asked.

"Yes, she does," he replied, with a slight hesitation. "Of course, she was still a child, you might say, then; but her mother was always full of praise for you, and you know what store she sets by the deceased's every word."

Yeltsova's words that I was not suitable for her Vera came to mind... "So *you* must have been suitable," I thought, sneaking sidelong glances at Priyimkov. He spent several hours with me. He's a very good, nice fellow, his talk is so modest, his look is so genial, it's impossible not to take a liking to him... but his mental capabilities have not developed since the time we knew him. I shall go and call on him without fail, perhaps even tomorrow. I'm extremely curious to see how Vera Nikolayevna has turned out.

You're probably laughing at me now, you villain, sitting at your director's desk: but I'll nonetheless write and tell you what impression she makes on me. Goodbye! Until the next letter.

Your P.B.

THIRD LETTER

From the same to the same

The village of M——oye, 16th June 1850

Well, old fellow, I've visited her, I've seen her. First of all I ought to inform you of an amazing fact: believe it or not, as you wish, but she has hardly changed at all either in face or in figure. When she came out to meet me, I all but gasped: quite simply, a girl of seventeen! Only the eyes are not like a girl's; but then even when she was young her eyes were not those of a child, they were too light. But the same calm, the same clarity, the voice the same, not a single wrinkle on her forehead, as if she had been lying in the snow somewhere all these years. But she's twenty-eight years old now, and she's had three children… I don't understand it! Please don't think I'm exaggerating because I'm biased; on the contrary, I didn't like this "changelessness" of hers at all.

A woman of twenty-eight, a wife and mother, ought not to resemble a little girl: she's not lived for nothing. She greeted me very cordially, but Priyimkov was simply delighted by my arrival: that kind fellow does nothing but look for a way to become attached to someone. Their house is very cosy and clean. Vera Nikolayevna was dressed like a little girl as well: all in white with a blue sash and a delicate gold chain around her neck. Her daughter is very sweet and not at all like her: she brings her grandmother to mind. In the drawing room above the sofa hangs a portrait of that strange woman, amazingly like her. I was struck by it as soon as I went in. She seemed to be looking at me sternly and closely. We sat ourselves down, reminisced about the old days, and little by little our conversation developed. I kept on involuntarily glancing at the gloomy portrait of Yeltsova. Vera Nikolayevna sat directly beneath it: that's her favourite place. Imagine my surprise: Vera Nikolayevna has still not yet read a single novel, or a single poem, in short, not a single – as she expresses it – invented work! This incomprehensible indifference to the most elevated pleasures of the mind made me angry. In a woman who is intelligent and, so far as I can judge, highly sensitive, it is simply unforgivable.

"Why is it," I asked, "that you've made a point of never reading such books?"

"I've not had occasion," she replied, "there's been no time."

"No time! I'm amazed! You at least," I continued, turning to Priyimkov, "might have given your wife a taste for it."

"With pleasure I'd..." Priyimkov began, but Vera Nikolayevna interrupted him.

"Don't put on a pretence: you're no great lover of poetry yourself."

"Not really of poetry, indeed," he began, "but novels, for example..."

"But what do you do, how do you keep yourselves occupied in the evenings?" I asked. "Do you play cards?"

"Sometimes we do," she replied, "but there's no shortage of things with which to occupy oneself. We read as well: there are good works besides poetry."

"Why do you attack poetry so?"

"I'm not attacking it: I've been accustomed from childhood not to read these invented works; that was the way Mother wanted it, and the longer I live, the more convinced I become that everything that Mother did, everything she said, was the truth, the holy truth."

"Well, as you wish, but I cannot agree with you: I'm convinced that you're depriving yourself to no purpose of the purest, the most legitimate pleasure. After all, you don't reject music, painting: why then do you reject poetry?"

"I don't reject it: I've not yet made its acquaintance – that's all."

"Then I'll take that upon myself! It wasn't for the rest of your life that your mother forbade your acquaintance with works of belles-lettres, was it?"

"No, as soon as I married, my mother withdrew any sort of prohibition from me; it didn't occur to me myself to read... how did you put it?... well, in short, to read novels."

I listened to Vera Nikolayevna in bewilderment: I had not expected this.

She looked at me with her calm gaze. Birds look like that when they're not afraid.

"I'll bring you a book!" I exclaimed. (The *Faust* that I had recently read came suddenly to mind.)

Vera Nikolayevna sighed quietly.

"It... it won't be George Sand?"* she asked, not without timidity.

"Ah, so you've heard of her? Well, perhaps even her, what's the harm?... No, I'll bring you another author. You haven't forgotten your German, have you?"

"No, I haven't."

"She speaks it like a German," Priyimkov joined in.

"That's fine then! I'll bring you... well, you'll see what an amazing thing I'll bring you."

"Alright then, I'll see. But now let's go into the garden; Natasha can't keep still otherwise."

She put on a round straw hat, a child's hat, exactly the same as the one her daughter put on, only a little bigger, and we set off into the garden. I walked alongside her. In the fresh air, in the shade of the tall limes, her face seemed to me even prettier, especially when she turned slightly and threw her head back to look at me from under the brim of the hat. Had it not been for Priyimkov walking behind us, had it not been for the little girl skipping ahead of us, I truly could have thought that I was not thirty-five, but twenty-three; that I was still only preparing to go to Berlin, particularly as the garden we were in was very like the garden on Yeltsova's estate too. I could not restrain myself and conveyed my impression to Vera Nikolayevna.

"Everyone tells me that I've changed very little outwardly," she replied, "but then I've remained the same inwardly too."

We went up to a small Chinese-style summer house.

"We didn't have a house like this in Osinovka," she said, "but pay no attention to its being so crumbling and faded, it's very nice and cool inside."

We went into the house. I looked around.

"Do you know what, Vera Nikolayevna?" I said. "Have a table and some chairs brought here for when I call. It really is wonderful here. Here I shall read you... Goethe's *Faust*... that's what I shall read you."

"Yes, there are no flies here," she remarked artlessly. "And when will you call?"

"The day after tomorrow."

"Alright," she said, "I'll give orders."

Natasha, who had come into the house with us, suddenly shrieked and leapt back, all pale.

"What's the matter?" asked Vera Nikolayevna.

"Oh, Mama," said the little girl, pointing into the corner, "look what a horrible spider!..."

Vera Nikolayevna glanced into the corner: a large, mottled spider was quietly crawling up the wall.

"What is there to be afraid of?" she said. "He doesn't bite, look."

And before I could stop her, she had picked the ugly insect up, let it run about on her palm and tossed it away.

"Why, how brave you are!" I exclaimed.

"Where's the bravery in that? It isn't a poisonous spider."

"You're evidently strong on natural history, like before; whereas I wouldn't have picked him up."

"There's no reason to be afraid of him," repeated Vera Nikolayevna.

Natasha looked at us both in silence and grinned.

"How like your mother she is!" I remarked.

"Yes," said Vera Nikolayevna with a smile of pleasure, "I'm very glad about that. God grant she resemble her not in looks alone!"

We were called in to lunch, and after lunch I left. (NB: The lunch was very nice and tasty – I'm noting that in brackets for you, you glutton!) Tomorrow I shall take them *Faust*. I'm afraid the old man Goethe and I might turn out a failure. I'll describe everything for you in detail.

Well, and what do you think now about all "the events herein"? Probably... that she's made a powerful impression on me, that I'm ready to fall in love, etc.? Nonsense, old fellow! It's time to move on. I've fooled around enough, that's it! You can't start life afresh at my age. And, what's more, it wasn't women like that I fancied even before... But then what women did I fancy!!

> I start to shudder – and my heart aches –
> My idols make me feel ashamed.*

In any event, I'm very glad we are neighbours, glad of the opportunity to see an intelligent, straightforward, bright creature; and what will happen next, that you'll learn all in good time.

Your P.B.

FOURTH LETTER

From the same to the same

The village of M——oye, 20th June 1850

The reading took place yesterday, my dear friend, and as to precisely how, the following points refer. First of all I hasten to say: unexpected success... that is, "success" isn't the word... Well, listen. I arrived for lunch. There were six of us at the table: her, Priyimkov, the daughter, the governess (an insignificant little white figure), me and some old German in a short brown tailcoat, clean, shaved, scrubbed, with the most meek and honest face, with a toothless smile and the smell of chicory coffee... all old Germans smell like that. We were introduced: this was a certain Schimmel, a German teacher from Priyimkov's neighbours, Prince Kh—— and his family. It seems that Vera Nikolayevna is well disposed towards him and invited him to be present at the reading. We had a late lunch and did not leave the table for a long time, then we took a walk. The weather was wonderful. It had rained in the morning and the wind had been making a noise, but by the evening everything had quietened down. She and I came out onto an open glade together. A large pink cloud hung high and light directly above the glade; streaks of grey stretched across it like smoke; at its very edge, now showing, now disappearing, there trembled a tiny star, while a little farther off could be seen the white sickle of the moon against the azure sky, lightly tinged with scarlet. I pointed this cloud out to Vera Nikolayevna.

"Yes," she said, "it's beautiful, but just look over here."

I looked round. A huge dark-blue storm cloud was rising up and blotting out the setting sun; in appearance it had the likeness of a fire-breathing mountain; its summit was thrown out across the sky in a broad cone; it was vividly edged all round with an ominous crimson glow which at one point, in the very centre, was breaking right through its heavy bulk, as though bursting out from a red-hot crater…

"Storm coming," remarked Priyimkov.

But I'm digressing from the point. In my last letter I forgot to tell you that when I got home from the Priyimkovs' I repented of having specified *Faust*; Schiller would have suited much better for the first occasion, if we were to be dealing with the Germans. I was particularly worried about the first scenes before the meeting with Gretchen; I wasn't happy as regards Mephistopheles either. But I was under the influence of *Faust* and could not willingly have read anything else. When it had already grown completely dark, we set off for the Chinese summer house; it had been put in order the day before. Directly opposite the door, in front of a small sofa, stood a circular table covered with a rug; armchairs and chairs were set out all around; on the table a lamp was burning. I sat down on the sofa and took out the book. Vera Nikolayevna took a seat in an armchair some distance away, not far from the door. Beyond the door, in the midst of the darkness, a green acacia branch stood out, rocking slightly, lit up by the lamp; a current of night air would occasionally flow into the room. Priyimkov sat down near me by the table, the German next to him. The governess had stayed in the house with Natasha. I made a short introductory speech: I mentioned the ancient legend of Dr Faustus, the significance of Mephistopheles, Goethe himself, and I asked to be stopped if anything should seem obscure. Then I cleared my throat… Priyimkov asked me whether I needed some sugared water, and all the signs were that he was very pleased with himself for putting this question to me. I refused. A deep silence fell. I began to read, without raising my eyes; I felt uncomfortable, my heart was pounding and my voice was shaking. The first exclamation of sympathy came from the German, and while the reading continued, he alone would break the silence… "Astonishing! Sublime!" he repeated, occasionally adding: "Now that is profound." Priyimkov, so far as I could make out, was bored: he did not understand German very well, and he himself confessed that he did not like poetry!… Well, that was up to him! While sitting at the table, I had almost tried to hint that the reading could manage without him, but had felt ashamed to do so. Vera Nikolayevna did not stir; I stole a couple of glances at her: her eyes were fixed directly and attentively upon me; her face seemed to me pale. After Faust's first meeting with Gretchen she moved forward from the back of her armchair, folded her arms and remained motionless in that position until the end. I sensed that Priyimkov was having a wretched time of it, and this at first turned me cold, but little by little I forgot about him, became excited and read with fervour, with passion… I was reading for Vera Nikolayevna alone: an inner voice told me that *Faust* was having an effect on her. When I finished (I omitted the Intermezzo: that bit already belongs in manner to the second part; and I tossed out part of 'The Night upon the Brocken' too)… when I finished, when that last "Heinrich!" had rung out, the German pronounced with emotion: "God! How beautiful!" Priyimkov, as if gladdened (the poor man!), jumped up, sighed and began thanking me for the pleasure I had given… But I did not reply to him: I was gazing at Vera Nikolayevna… I wanted to hear what she would say. She got up, took some indecisive steps towards the door, stood for a while on the threshold and went quietly out into the garden. I rushed after her. She had already managed to move several steps away; the whiteness of her dress could just be seen in the dense shadow.

"Well, then," I cried, "didn't you enjoy it?"

She stopped.

"Can you leave that book with me?" her voice rang out.

"I'll give it to you as a gift, Vera Nikolayevna, if you wish to have it."

"I'm grateful!" she replied, and disappeared.

Priyimkov and the German came up to me.

"How amazingly warm!" remarked Priyimkov. "Airless even. But where has my wife gone?"

"Home, it appears," I replied.

"I think so, it'll soon be time for dinner," he said. "You read superbly," he added after a slight pause.

"Vera Nikolayevna appears to have enjoyed *Faust*," I said.

"Without doubt!" exclaimed Priyimkov.

"Oh, but of course!" Schimmel chimed in.

We arrived at the house.

"Where's the mistress?" enquired Priyimkov of a maid who was coming towards us.

"She's gone to her room."

Priyimkov went off to the bedroom.

I went out onto the terrace along with Schimmel. The old man raised his eyes to the sky.

"How many stars!" he said slowly, after taking some snuff. "And they're all worlds," he added, before sniffing a second time.

I did not think it necessary to answer him and only looked up in silence. A secret perplexity weighed upon my soul. The stars seemed to me to be looking at us seriously. After five minutes or so Priyimkov appeared and called us into the dining room. Soon Vera Nikolayevna came in too. We sat down.

"Just look at Verochka," said Priyimkov to me.

I glanced at her.

"What? Don't you notice anything?"

I did indeed notice a change in her face, but I replied, I don't know why: "No, nothing."

"Her eyes are red," continued Priyimkov.

I remained silent.

"Just imagine, I've gone upstairs to her room, and I find her crying. It's a long time since she's been like this. I can tell you when the last time she cried was: when our Sasha passed away. There's what you've done with your *Faust*!" he added, with a smile.

"So now, Vera Nikolayevna," I began, "you can see that I was right when…"

"I didn't expect this," she interrupted me, "but still, God knows whether you're right. Perhaps Mother forbade me to read such books for the very reason that she knew…"

Vera Nikolayevna stopped.

"That she knew?" I repeated. "Go on."

"To what end? I'm ashamed as it is: what was it I was crying about? But then you and I will discuss it further. There was a lot I didn't understand at all."

"But why didn't you stop me?"

"I understood all the words and their meaning, but…"

She did not finish what she was saying and fell into thought. At that instant there came from the garden the rustling of leaves suddenly shaken by the rising wind. Vera Nikolayevna shuddered and turned to face the wide-open window.

"I told you there'd be a storm!" exclaimed Priyimkov. "But Verochka, why is it you're shuddering like that?"

She glanced at him in silence. A weak flash of distant lightning was reflected mysteriously on her immobile face.

"All thanks to *Faust*," continued Priyimkov. "After dinner it'll have to be straight to bed… isn't that so, Mr Schimmel?"

"After spiritual pleasure, physical rest is as salutary as it is beneficial," said the kind German, and drank down a glass of vodka.

We dispersed immediately after dinner. Saying goodnight to Vera Nikolayevna, I shook her hand: her hand was cold. I went to the room that I had been given and stood for a long time at the window before undressing and getting into bed. Priyimkov's prediction had come true: the storm had arrived and broken out. I listened to the noise of the wind, the knocking and slapping of the rain, watched as, with every flash of lightning, the church, built nearby above the lake, would be now suddenly black against a white background, now white against black, now swallowed up by the gloom once again... But my thoughts were far away. I was thinking of Vera Nikolayevna, thinking of what she would say to me when she had read *Faust* for herself, thinking of her tears, recalling how she had listened...

The storm had already passed long before – the stars had begun to shine, everything had fallen quiet all around. Some bird I did not know was singing in different voices, repeating one and the same figure several times in succession. Its resonant, solitary voice sounded strange in the midst of the profound silence; and still I did not go to bed...

The next morning I went down into the drawing room earlier than anyone, and stopped in front of the portrait of Yeltsova. "Well, you've got to accept it," I thought, with a secret feeling of mocking triumph, "you see, I've read your daughter a forbidden book!" Suddenly I imagined... you've probably noticed that eyes *en face* always seem to be directed straight at the viewer... but on this occasion I really did imagine that the old woman had trained them on me in reproach.

I turned away, went up to the window, and saw Vera Nikolayevna. With an umbrella on her shoulder, with a light white scarf on her head, she was walking through the garden. I immediately went out of the house and greeted her.

"I've been awake all night," she told me, "I've got a headache; I came out into the air – perhaps it will pass."

"Surely it's not because of yesterday's reading?" I asked.

"Of course: I'm not used to it. In that book of yours there are things I simply can't escape from; I think they're what is burning my head so," she added, putting her hand to her forehead.

"That's splendid," I said, "but this is the bad part: I'm afraid this insomnia and headache might dispel your desire to read such things."

"Do you think so?" she said, and, in passing, broke off a wild jasmine twig. "God knows! It seems to me that anybody who once steps onto this road will never turn back again."

Suddenly she threw the twig aside.

"Come and sit down in this gazebo," she continued, "and please, until I myself begin the conversation with you, don't mention... that book to me." (It was as if she were afraid to pronounce the name *Faust*.)

We went into the gazebo and sat down.

"I shan't talk to you about *Faust*," I began, "but you'll allow me to congratulate you and tell you that I envy you."

"You envy me?"

"Yes, with your soul, as I now know you, how much enjoyment you have ahead of you! There are great poets besides Goethe: Shakespeare, Schiller, and our own Pushkin too... you must get to know him as well."

She was silent and drew lines in the sand with the umbrella.

Oh my friend, Semyon Nikolayich, if you could have seen how pretty she was at that moment: pale almost to the point of transparency, bending slightly, tired, inwardly disturbed – and nonetheless clear as the sky! I talked, talked for a long time, then fell quiet – and just sat there in silence gazing at her...

She did not raise her eyes, and continued either drawing with the umbrella or rubbing out what she had drawn. Suddenly the nimble steps of a child were heard: Natasha ran into the gazebo. Vera Nikolayevna straightened up, rose, and, to my surprise, embraced her daughter with a kind of impetuous tenderness... That is not her way. Then Priyimkov appeared. The grey-haired but punctilious baby, Schimmel, had left before first light so as not to miss a lesson. We went to have tea.

However, I'm tired; it's time to finish this letter. It must seem to you nonsensical, confused. I feel confused myself. I'm out of sorts. I don't know what's wrong with me. I keep on imagining a small room with bare walls, a lamp, a wide-open door; the scent and freshness of the night, and there, beside the door, an attentive young face, light, white clothes... I understand now why I wanted to marry her: I evidently wasn't as stupid before the trip to Berlin as I'd thought up until now. Yes, Semyon Nikolayich, your friend finds himself in a strange spiritual state. This will all pass, I know... and if it doesn't pass – well, what of it? – it doesn't pass. But all the same I'm pleased with myself: firstly, I spent an astounding evening; and secondly, if I have awakened this spirit, who can blame me? The old woman, Yeltsova, is nailed to the wall and has to remain silent. The old woman!... The details of her life are not all known to me, but I do know that she ran away from her father's house – not for nothing, evidently, was she born of an Italian mother. She wanted insurance for her daughter... We'll see.

I'm throwing down the pen. Please think whatever you like of me, you sardonic fellow, but don't mock me in writing. You and I are old friends and ought to spare one another. Goodbye!

Your P.B.

FIFTH LETTER

From the same to the same

The village of M——oye, 26th July 1850

I've not written to you for a long time, dear Semyon Nikolayich, more than a month, I think. There have been things to write about, but idleness got the better of me. To tell the truth, I've hardly thought about you all this time. But I can conclude from your last letter to me that you are making assumptions about me that are unjust, that is, not entirely just. You think I am enamoured of Vera (I feel awkward somehow calling her Vera Nikolayevna); you're mistaken. Of course, I see her often, I am extremely fond of her... but who wouldn't be fond of her? I'd like to see you in my place. An amazing creature! Instant perspicacity alongside the inexperience of a child, clear common sense and an innate feeling for beauty, constant aspiration towards truth, towards the elevated, and understanding of everything, even vice, even the ridiculous – and above all this, like the white wings of an angel, such feminine charm... Well, it's no use denying it! She and I have read a lot and talked a lot over the course of the month. Reading with her is a pleasure such as I have never before experienced. It's as if you're discovering new countries. She does not go into raptures about anything: any sort of noise is alien to her; she is all quietly aglow when she likes something, and her face adopts an expression of such nobility and goodness... specifically goodness. From her earliest childhood Vera has not known what a lie is: she has become accustomed to truth, she breathes it, and for that reason truth alone seems natural to her in poetry too; she recognizes it immediately, without difficulty or strain, like a familiar face… a great advantage and good fortune! One cannot but think well of her mother for that. How many times have I thought, looking at Vera: yes, Goethe is right:

> A good man in his unclear aspiration
> Is always conscious where the true path lies.*

One thing is annoying: her husband keeps hanging around. (Please don't laugh a stupid laugh, don't profane our pure friendship even in thought.) He is just as capable of understanding poetry as I am disposed to play the flute, but he does not want to fall behind his wife, he wants to be enlightened as well. Sometimes she exasperates me herself; some mood will suddenly descend upon her: she doesn't want to read or talk, she works at her tambour, spends time with Natasha, with the housekeeper, runs all of a sudden to the kitchen, or simply sits with her arms tightly crossed and keeps looking out of the window, or else starts playing old maid with the nanny… I've noticed that in these instances she shouldn't be bothered, it's better to wait for her to come to you herself, to start a conversation or to pick up a book. There is a great deal of independence in her, and I'm very glad of it. Sometimes, you remember, in the days of our youth, some girl would repeat to you as best she could your very own words, and you'd be enraptured by this echo and maybe worship it, until you got to the bottom of what was going on; but this one… no: this one goes her own way. She won't take anything on trust; you won't intimidate her with authority; she won't think of arguing, but neither will she yield. She and I have discussed *Faust* on more than one occasion: yet – it's a strange thing! – she says nothing herself about Gretchen, but only listens to what I'll say to her. Mephistopheles frightens her not as a devil, but as "something that might be found in anyone"… Those are her own words. I began to explain to her that we call this "something" reflection; but she didn't understand the word reflection in the German sense: she only knows the French *réflexion* and is accustomed to thinking it beneficial. Our relationship is astonishing! From a certain point of view I can say that I exert a great influence on her and am, as it were, educating her; but she too, without noticing it herself, is in many respects changing me for the better. Only thanks to her, for example, have I recently discovered what a huge amount of the conventional, the rhetorical there is in many fine and well-known poetical works. What she remains cold towards is, in my eyes, already under suspicion. Yes, I've become better, clearer. To be near her, to meet with her and remain the person you used to be is impossible.

What will come of all this, then? you ask. And I really do think nothing will. I shall spend the time until September most pleasantly, and then I shall leave. Life will seem dark and dull to me for the first months... I'll get used to it. I know how dangerous any sort of liaison is between a man and a young woman, how one feeling is replaced, unnoticed, by another... I would be able to break away, if I were not conscious that we are both perfectly calm. Once, it's true, something strange happened between us. I don't know how and in consequence of what – I seem to recall we were reading *Onegin** – but I kissed her hand. She moved away a little, fastened her gaze upon me (I've not seen such a gaze in anyone but her: there is pensiveness in it, and attention, and a sort of severity)... suddenly she blushed, got up, and left. I didn't manage to be alone with her again that day. She avoided me and for a good four hours played trumps with her husband, the nanny and the governess! The next morning she invited me to go into the garden. We walked through it all the way to the lake. Without turning towards me, she suddenly whispered quietly: "Please, don't do that in future!" and immediately began telling me something... I felt very shamed.

I must admit that her image never leaves my mind, and my intention when I began writing this letter to you was little more than to have the opportunity to think and talk about her. I can hear the snorting of horses and the clatter of their hooves: it's my carriage that's been made ready. I'm going to see them. My coachman no longer asks me where to drive now when I get into the carriage – he takes me straight to the Priyimkovs'. Two versts before you reach their village, on a sharp bend in the road, their house suddenly peeps out from behind a birch grove... My heart fills with joy every time, just as soon as her windows gleam out in the distance. Not for nothing does Schimmel (that harmless old man occasionally visits them; Prince Kh—— and his family they have seen, thank God, only once)... does Schimmel say with his characteristically modest solemnity, indicating the house where Vera lives: "That is the abode of peace!" An angel of peace certainly has taken up residence in that house...

So cloak me with your wing and calm
The agitation of my breast –

The shade will be as healing balm
And set my captive soul at rest...*

But enough, however; otherwise God knows what you'll think. Until the next time... Whatever will I write the next time? Goodbye! Incidentally, she'll never say: "goodbye", but always: "well, goodbye". I'm terribly fond of that.

Your P.B.

PS: I don't know whether I ever told you that she knows I asked to marry her.

SIXTH LETTER

From the same to the same

The village of M——oye, 10th August 1850

Admit it, you expect from me a letter that is either despairing or rapturous… Nothing of the sort! My letter will be like all the other letters. Nothing new has happened, nor does it seem it can happen. A few days ago we went out boating on the lake. I'll describe the trip for you. There were three of us: her, Schimmel and me. I don't understand what it is that makes her invite that old man so often. The Kh—— family are grumbling about him, saying he has started to neglect his lessons. On this occasion, though, he was amusing. Priyimkov didn't come with us: he had a headache. The weather was splendid, cheerful: big white clouds, looking as if they'd been ripped apart across the blue sky, brilliance everywhere, a rustling in the trees, the splashing and slapping of the water by the shore, fleeting golden ripples on the waves, fresh air and sunshine! At first the German and I rowed; then we raised the sail and sped away. The bow of the boat really started diving, and behind the stern the wake hissed and foamed. She sat down at the rudder and began to steer; she had tied a scarf on her head: a hat would have been carried away; her curls were torn out from beneath it and beat softly at the air. She held the rudder firmly with her tanned little hand, and smiled at the spray that occasionally flew into her face. I curled up in the bottom of the boat, not far from her feet; the German took out his pipe, lit up his tobacco, and – just imagine – began singing in quite a pleasant bass voice.

First he sang the old song '*Freu't euch des Lebens*',* then an aria from *The Magic Flute*, then a romance by the name of 'The Alphabet of Love' – '*Das A-B-C der Liebe*'. This song goes – with decent comic verses, naturally – through the whole alphabet, beginning with "A, B, C, D – when you I see!", and ending with "X, Y and Z – bow down your head!". He sang all the couplets through with a sensitive expression; but it had to be seen, the way he screwed up his left eye roguishly at the word: "head". Vera burst out laughing and wagged her finger at him. I remarked that, so far as I could tell, Mr Schimmel was nobody's fool in his day. "Quite right, and I could stick up for myself!" he said pompously, knocking the ash from the pipe out onto his palm and, dipping his fingers into his tobacco pouch, he bit rakishly with his side teeth on the mouthpiece of his pipe stem. "When I was a student," he added, "oh-ho-ho!" He said nothing more. But what an "oh-ho-ho" it was! Vera asked him to sing a student song of some sort, and he sang her '*Knaster, den gelben*', but the last note was out of tune. He really had got quite carried away. Meanwhile the wind had strengthened, quite big waves had started to roll, the boat was tilting slightly, and swallows had begun darting low around us. We reset the sail and started tacking. The wind suddenly shifted, we didn't have time to right ourselves, a wave splashed over the side, and the boat became quite waterlogged. At this point the German showed his mettle; he tore the rope away from me and set the sail properly, saying as he did so: "This is how it's done in Cuxhaven!" – "*So macht man's in Cuxhaven!*"

Vera was probably frightened, because she turned pale, but, as is her wont, did not utter a word, gathered up her dress and put the tips of her feet on the boat's transom. A poem by Goethe suddenly came into my head (for some time I've been absolutely plagued by him)... do you remember: 'On the waters there sparkle a thousand rocking stars',* and I recited it out loud. When I reached the line: "Eyes, my eyes, why sink you down?" she raised her eyes a little (I was sitting lower than her:

her gaze fell on me from above) and looked into the distance for a long time, squinting because of the wind... Light rain was upon us in a moment and bubbles began to jump across the water. I offered her my coat: she threw it over her shoulders. We put in to the shore – not at the landing stage – and reached the house on foot. I led her by the arm. It was as if I constantly wanted to say something to her; but I was silent. I seem to recall, however, that I did ask her why she always sat beneath Mrs Yeltsova's portrait when she was at home, like a fledgling under its mother's wing. "Your simile is very apt," she said, "I should never wish to come out from under her wing." "Would not wish to come out and be at liberty?" I asked again. She made no reply.

I don't know why I've recounted this outing to you – perhaps just because it has remained in my memory as one of the brightest events of the past days, although in reality it's not much of an event. I was so gratified and wordlessly cheerful, and tears, easy, happy tears were just begging to be shed.

Yes! Imagine, the next day, passing by a gazebo in the garden, I suddenly hear a pleasant, resonant, female voice, and it's singing: "*Freu't euch des Lebens...*" I glanced into the gazebo: it was Vera. "Bravo!" I exclaimed, "I never knew you had such a splendid voice!" She became embarrassed and fell silent. Joking apart, she has an excellent, powerful soprano. Yet I don't think she even suspected she had a good voice. How many untouched riches are still hidden within her! She does not know herself. But isn't it true that nowadays such a woman is a rarity?

12th August

We had the strangest conversation yesterday. First we talked about ghosts. Imagine: she believes in them and says she has her reasons for doing so. Priyimkov, who was sitting there too, lowered his eyes and shook his head as if in confirmation of her words. I tried to start questioning her, but soon noticed that she found this conversation unpleasant. We began to talk about the imagination, about the power of the imagination. I told how in my youth, when I dreamt a lot about happiness (a common pastime for people who have not been, or are not lucky in life), I dreamt among other things of what bliss it would be to spend some weeks in Venice with a woman I loved. I thought about this so often, especially at night, that little by little a whole picture formed in my head, which I could call up before me at will: I had only to close my eyes. This is what I imagined: night-time, the moon, the light from the moon, white and gentle, the scent… you're thinking "of lemon"? No, of vanilla, the scent of cactus, a broad expanse of smooth water, a flat island overgrown with olive-trees; on the island, right by the shore's edge, a small marble house with wide-open windows; music can be heard, God knows from where; in the house there are trees with dark leaves and the light of a half-shaded lamp; a heavy velvet mantle with a gold fringe has been draped out of one window and has one end lying on the water; and *he* and *she* are sitting next to one another, leaning on the mantle, gazing into the distance to where Venice can be seen. I could imagine it all so clearly, as though I had seen it all with my own eyes. She heard out my fantasies and said that she too often dreamed, but that her dreams were of a different kind: she either imagined herself on the plains of Africa with some traveller, or seeking out the trail of Franklin* in the Arctic Ocean; she could vividly picture all the deprivations she had to suffer, all the difficulties with which she was obliged to struggle…

"You've read too many travel books," remarked her husband.

"Perhaps," she said, "but if you're going to dream, who wants to dream about the unrealizable?"

"But why not?" I joined in. "What has the poor old unrealizable done wrong?"

"I expressed myself wrongly," she said, "what I meant was: who wants to dream about themselves, about their own happiness? There's no point in thinking about it; if it doesn't come, why chase after it? It's like good health: when you don't notice it, that means you've got it."

Those words surprised me. Within this woman is a great spirit, believe me... From Venice the conversation turned to Italy, to the Italians. Priyimkov left the room, Vera and I remained alone.

"In your veins too there flows Italian blood," I remarked.

"Yes," she said, "would you like me to show you a portrait of my grandmother?"

"If you'd be so kind."

She went to her study and from there she brought quite a large gold locket. Opening this locket, I saw superbly painted miniature portraits of Yeltsova's father and his wife – the peasant from Albano. I was struck by Vera's grandfather's resemblance to his daughter. The only thing was that his features, fringed with a white cloud of powder, seemed even more severe, pointed and sharp, while in his little yellow eyes there shone a certain sullen obstinacy. But what a face the Italian had! Voluptuous, open, like a rose in full bloom, with large, moist, prominent eyes and rosy lips, smiling in self-satisfaction! The fine, sensual nostrils seemed to be quivering and dilating as after recent kisses; the dark-complexioned cheeks positively radiated sultry good health, the luxuriance of youth and feminine strength... That brow had never thought seriously, and thank God for it! She was drawn in her Albano costume; the painter (a master!) had placed a vine twig in her hair, which was as black as pitch, with bright-grey highlights: this Bacchic adornment could not have been better suited to the expression on her face. And do you know who I was reminded of by this face? My Manon Lescaut in the black frame. And most surprising of all is that, looking at this portrait, I remembered that, despite the utter dissimilarity of outlines, there is at times in Vera a glimpse of something resembling this smile, this look...

Yes, I say it again: neither she herself, nor anybody else on earth yet knows all that is hidden inside her…

Incidentally! Just before her daughter's wedding Yeltsova related the whole of her life to her, the death of her own mother etc., probably with an instructive aim. Vera was particularly affected by what she heard about her grandfather, about this mysterious Ladanov. Is it perhaps because of this that she believes in ghosts? It's strange! She is herself so pure and bright, yet she fears everything that is gloomy, of the netherworld, and she believes in it…

However, enough. Why write all this? But then, since it's already been written, let it be sent off to you too.

Your P.B.

SEVENTH LETTER

From the same to the same

The village of M——oye, 22nd August

I take up my pen ten days after the last letter... Oh my friend, I can conceal myself no more... How wretched I am! How I love her! You can imagine with what a bitter shudder I write that fateful word. I am not a boy, not even a young man; I am no longer of an age when deceiving another is almost impossible, while deceiving oneself is no trouble at all. I know everything and can see clearly. I know that I'm almost forty, that she is another man's wife, that she loves her husband; I know very well that from the unfortunate feeling that has taken hold of me I can expect nothing other than secret torments and the final squandering of my life forces – I know all of this, I hope for nothing and want nothing; but that does not make things any easier for me. About a month ago I had already begun to notice that the attraction she held for me was becoming stronger and stronger. This in part embarrassed, in part even pleased me... Yet could I have expected that the things for which, just like youth, there had seemed to be no return would all be repeated for me? But what am I saying! I never loved like this, no, never! Manon Lescauts, Fretillons* – these were my idols. Such idols are easily smashed; but now... only now have I learnt what it means to fall in love with a woman. I feel ashamed even to talk about it; but it is so. I feel ashamed... Love is, after all, egotism; and to be an egotist at my age is impermissible: you cannot live for yourself at thirty-seven; you should live usefully, with a purpose on earth, carry out your duty, your business. And I had begun to set about my work... But now everything has been scattered again, as if by a whirlwind! Now I understand what I was writing to you about in my first letter; I understand what test I was lacking. How suddenly this blow has fallen on my head! I am standing and gazing senselessly forward: a black curtain hangs just in front of my eyes; my soul is wretched and fearful! I can restrain myself, I am outwardly calm, not only for others, even in private; I really can't rave, after all, as if I were a boy! But the worm has crawled into my heart and is sucking at it day and night. How will it end? Until now I had pined and worried in her absence, and immediately calmed down in her presence... Now I am troubled in her presence – that is what frightens me. Oh my friend, how hard it is to be ashamed of one's tears, to conceal them!... Youth alone can be permitted to cry; it alone is suited by tears...

I cannot reread this letter; it has been torn from me involuntarily, like a groan. I cannot add anything, relate anything... Give me time: I'll come to my senses, get a grip on my soul, I'll speak to you like a man, but just now I should like to lean my head on your breast and...

O, Mephistopheles! You too fail to help me. I stopped on purpose, on purpose I tried to rouse the ironic vein within me, to remind myself of how ridiculous and morbid these complaints, these outpourings would seem to me in a year, in six months... No, Mephistopheles is powerless, and his tooth is blunted... Goodbye.

Your P.B.

EIGHTH LETTER

From the same to the same

The village of M——oye, 8th September 1850

My dear friend, Semyon Nikolayich!

You took my last letter too much to heart. You know how I'm always inclined to exaggerate my sensations. It happens with me involuntarily somehow: a woman's nature! It will, of course, pass with the years; but I admit with a sigh, I have still not reformed as yet. And so relax. I will not deny the impression made on me by Vera, but then again I'll say there is nothing unusual in all of this. There is absolutely no need for you to come here, as you write. To gallop a thousand versts for God knows what reason – that would simply be madness! But I am very grateful to you for this new proof of your friendship and, believe me, shall never forget it. Your journey here is also inappropriate because I myself intend to leave soon for St Petersburg. Sitting on your sofa, I shall tell you many things, whereas I really don't feel like it now: who knows, I might say too much again and confuse matters. I'll write to you once more just before I leave. And so until we meet again soon, be well and happy, and don't grieve too much over the lot of

Your devoted P.B.

NINTH LETTER

From the same to the same

The village of P——oye, 10th March 1853

I've been a long time replying to your letter; I've been thinking about it all these days. I felt that you were prompted to it not by idle curiosity, but by true friendly concern; yet I nonetheless wavered: should I follow your advice, should I carry out your wish? Finally I've made up my mind; I shall tell you everything. Whether my confession will relieve me, as you suppose, I don't know; but it seems to me that I have no right to conceal from you the thing that has changed my life for ever; it seems to me that I would even be at fault... alas! even more at fault before that unforgettable, dear shade, if I did not entrust our sad secret to the only heart I still hold dear. Perhaps you alone on earth remember about Vera, and you make flippant and false judgements about her; that I cannot allow. And so learn everything. Alas! It can all be conveyed in two words. What there was between us flashed by in an instant like lightning, and, like lightning, brought death and ruin...

More than two years have gone by since she passed away, since I settled here in this backwater, which I shall not leave now until the end of my days, and yet everything is so clear in my memory, my wounds are still so raw, my grief so bitter...

I shall not be complaining. Complaints, in irritating, do alleviate sorrow, but not mine. I shall be recounting.

You remember my last letter – that letter in which I thought to dispel your fears and advised against your setting out from

St Petersburg? You were suspicious of its forced nonchalance, you did not believe we would meet again soon: you were right. On the eve of that day when I wrote to you, I had learnt that I was loved.

Tracing these words, I have realized how difficult it will be for me to continue my story to the end. The persistent thought of her death will torment me with redoubled force, I shall be seared by these memories... But I shall try to control myself and will either give up writing or not say an unnecessary word.

This is how I learnt that Vera loved me. First of all I should tell you (and you will believe me) that until that day I suspected absolutely nothing. True, she had started sometimes falling into a reverie, which had never been the case with her previously, but I did not understand why this was happening to her. Finally, one day, on the 7th of September – a memorable day for me – this is what happened. You know how I loved her and how wretched I was. I wandered about like a shadow, I couldn't keep still. I meant to stay at home, but couldn't bear it and set off to see her. I found her alone in the study. Priyimkov was not at home: he had gone off hunting. When I went in to Vera she looked at me intently and did not reply to my bow. She was sitting by the window; on her lap lay a book which I recognized at once: it was my *Faust*. Her face expressed fatigue. I sat down opposite her. She asked me to read out loud the scene between Faust and Gretchen where she asks him whether he believes in God. I took the book and began reading. When I had finished, I glanced at her. With her head leaning against the back of the armchair and her arms crossed on her breast, she was still looking at me just as intently.

I don't know why, but my heart suddenly began pounding.

"What have you done to me!" she said in a slow voice.

"What?" I asked in confusion.

"Yes, what have you done to me!" she repeated.

"Do you mean," I began, "why did I persuade you to read such books?"

She stood up in silence and went to leave the room. I gazed after her.

On the threshold she stopped and turned back to me.

"I love you," she said, "that's what you've done to me."

The blood rushed to my head...

"I love you, I'm in love with you," repeated Vera.

She left and closed the door behind her. I will not begin to describe to you what happened to me then. I remember I went out into the garden, made my way into its depths, leant up against a tree, and how long I spent standing there, I cannot say. It was as if I had frozen; every so often a feeling of bliss ran in waves through my heart... No, I won't begin to speak about that. I was summoned from my numbed state by Priyimkov's voice; someone had been sent to tell him that I had come: he had returned from the hunt and had been looking for me. He was astonished to find me alone in the garden, hatless, and he led me into the house. "My wife's in the drawing room," he said, "let's go and join her." You can imagine the feelings with which I crossed the threshold of the drawing room. Vera was sitting in the corner at her tambour; I stole a glance at her and afterwards did not raise my eyes for a long time. To my surprise, she appeared calm – in what she said, in the sound of her voice, no alarm could be heard. Finally I made up my mind to look at her. Our gazes met. She flushed slightly and bent over her canvas. I began observing her. She seemed to be bewildered; a mirthless smile occasionally touched her lips.

Priyimkov left the room. She suddenly raised her head and asked me quite loudly:

"What do you intend to do now?"

I became confused and hurriedly replied in a hollow voice that I intended to fulfil the duty of an honest man and withdraw, "because," I added, "I love you, Vera Nikolayevna, you probably noticed that long ago." She again bent down towards the canvas and fell into thought.

"I must have a talk with you," she said. "Come this evening after tea to our summer house... you know, where you read *Faust*."

She said this so distinctly that even now I cannot comprehend how Priyimkov, who was entering the room at that very instant, did not hear anything. That day passed quietly, agonizingly quietly. Vera sometimes gazed around with such an expression, it was as if she were wondering whether she was dreaming. And at the same time there was resolve written on her face. While I... I could not come to my senses. Vera loves me! These words were turning round continually in my mind; but I did not understand them – I did not understand either myself, or her. I did not believe such unexpected, such staggering good fortune; it took an effort to recall what had passed, and I too gazed and spoke as though in a dream...

After tea, when I was already beginning to think how I might slip out of the house unnoticed, she herself suddenly announced that she wanted to go for a walk and suggested I accompany her. I rose, picked up my hat and set off after her. I did not dare to begin speaking, I was scarcely breathing, I was waiting for the first word from her, waiting for confessions; but she was silent. We reached the Chinese summer house in silence, we entered it in silence, and at that point – I still don't know, can't understand how it happened – we suddenly found ourselves in one another's arms. Some unseen force had thrown me towards her and her towards me. In the dying light of the day her face, with its curls tossed back, was lit up instantaneously with a smile of abandon and languor, and our lips merged in a kiss...

That kiss was our first and our last.

Vera suddenly tore herself out of my arms and, with an expression of horror in her widened eyes, she reeled away from me...

"Look behind you," she said to me, her voice trembling, "do you see anything?"

I turned around quickly.

"No, nothing. Can you see something, then?"

"I can't now, but I did see something."

She was breathing deeply and slowly.

"Whom? What?"

"My mother," she said slowly, and her whole body began to tremble.

I shivered as well, as though I had come over cold; I suddenly felt awful, like a criminal. And was I not indeed a criminal at that moment?

"Enough!" I began. "What is all this? Tell me instead..."

"No, for God's sake, no!" she interrupted, taking her head in her hands. "It's madness... I'm going mad... This is no joking matter – this is death... Goodbye..."

I reached out my arms to her.

"Stop for a moment, for God's sake," I exclaimed in an involuntary rush. I didn't know what I was saying and could hardly stay on my feet. "For God's sake... I mean, this is cruel."

She glanced at me.

"Tomorrow, tomorrow evening," she said, "not today, I beg you... leave today... tomorrow evening come to the garden gate beside the lake. I'll be there, I'll come... I swear to you, I'll come," she added passionately, and her eyes shone, "whoever might try to stop me, I swear it! I'll tell you everything, only let me go today."

And before I could say a word, she had vanished.

Shaken to the core, I stayed where I was. My head was spinning. Through the mad joy that was filling my entire being there stole a feeling of melancholy... I looked around. The damp, God-forsaken room in which I stood seemed terrible to me with its low vault and its dark walls.

I went outside and directed my heavy steps towards the house. Vera was waiting for me on the terrace; she entered the house as soon as I came near and immediately withdrew to her bedroom.

I left.

How I spent the night and the following day until the evening – that cannot be conveyed. I only remember that I lay face down with my face hidden in my hands, recalling her smile before the kiss and whispering: "There she is, at last..."

I also recalled the words of Yeltsova, conveyed to me by Vera. She had said to her one day: "You're like ice: until you melt, you're as strong as stone, but when you melt, not even a trace of you will be left."

This is what else came to mind: Vera and I were once discussing what was meant by know-how, talent.

"I know how to do only one thing," she said, "remain silent until the last moment."

At the time I didn't understand at all.

"But what does her fright mean?..." I wondered. "Surely she didn't really see Yeltsova? Imagination!" I thought, and once more gave myself up to sensations of expectation.

That same day I wrote – with what ideas, I dread to recall – that devious letter to you.

In the evening – the sun was not yet setting – I was already standing some fifty paces from the garden gate among some tall, dense willows on the shore of the lake. I had come from home on foot. I confess, to my shame: fear, the most pusillanimous fear, filled my breast, I was constantly giving a start... but I did not feel repentant. Hidden among the branches I gazed persistently at the gate. It did not open. Now the sun had set, it had become dark; the stars had already come out, and the sky had turned black. Nobody appeared. I was racked by fever. Night had fallen. I could bear it no longer. I emerged cautiously from the willows and stole up to the gate. All was quiet in the garden. I called to Vera in a whisper, called a second time, a third... No voice responded. Another half-hour passed, an hour passed; it became completely dark. Waiting had exhausted me; I pulled the gate towards me, opened it at a stroke, and on tiptoe, like a thief, moved towards the house. I stopped in the shadow of the limes.

Almost all the windows in the house were lit up; people were going backwards and forwards through the rooms. This surprised me: my watch, so far as I could distinguish by the dim light of the stars, was showing half-past eleven. Suddenly there was a clatter beyond the house: a carriage was driving out of the courtyard.

"Guests, evidently," I thought. Having lost all hope of seeing Vera, I made my way out of the garden and set off for home at a rapid pace. The September night was dark, but warm and windless. The feeling that had all but overwhelmed me, not so much of annoyance as of sadness, was gradually dispelled, and I arrived home a little tired from walking fast, but calmed by the silence of the night, happy and almost cheerful. I went into my bedroom, sent Timofei away, threw myself onto the bed without undressing, and sank into thought.

At first my dreams were comforting; but soon I noticed a strange change in myself. I began to feel some secret, gnawing anguish, some profound inner disquiet. I could not understand why this was happening; but I was starting to feel dread and weariness, as if threatened by misfortune close by, as if somebody dear were suffering at that moment and calling on me for help. On the table burned the small, still flame of a wax candle, the ticking of a pendulum was heavy and measured. I propped up my head with my hand and started gazing into the empty semi-darkness of my lonely room. I thought of Vera, and inside me my soul began to ache: everything I had so rejoiced at now seemed to me, as, indeed, it ought to have done, misfortune, inescapable ruin. The feeling of anguish grew and grew within me, I could lie down no longer; I suddenly imagined once more that someone was calling me in an imploring voice... I raised my head a little and gave a start; so it was, I wasn't deceiving myself: a pitiful cry sped to me from afar and clung, weakly tinkling, to the black panes of the windows. I grew terrified. I leapt up from the bed, opened the window wide. A distinct groan burst into the room and seemed to circle above me. Quite cold in horror, I heard its final, dying modulations. It was as if somebody were being slaughtered in the distance, and as if the unfortunate were begging in vain for mercy. Whether it was an owl that had cried out in the copse, or some other creature that had emitted this groan, I was not aware at the time, but, like Mazepa to Kochubei,* I called out in reply to this ominous sound.

"Vera, Vera!" I exclaimed. "Is that you calling me?"

Timofei appeared before me, sleepy and bewildered.

I recovered myself, drank a glass of water, moved into another room; but sleep did not come to me. My heart was beating painfully inside me, albeit not fast. I was no longer able to give myself up to dreams of happiness; I no longer dared believe in it.

Before lunch the next day I set off to call on Priyimkov. He greeted me with a troubled face.

"My wife is ill," he began, "she's in bed; I've had the doctor here."

"What's the matter with her?"

"I can't understand it. Yesterday evening she was going out into the garden, then suddenly returned, beside herself with fright. The maid ran to fetch me. I go and ask my wife, 'What's the matter with you?' She doesn't answer, but goes to bed straight away; during the night she became delirious. She was saying God knows what in her delirium, she mentioned you. The maid told me an astonishing thing: Verochka is supposed to have seen the ghost of her late mother in the garden, supposed to have had the impression that it was walking towards her with its arms open wide."

You can imagine what I felt at those words.

"Of course it's nonsense," Priyimkov continued, "but I must admit that unusual things of this sort have happened with my wife before."

"And tell me, is Vera Nikolayevna very unwell?"

"Yes, she's unwell: she was bad in the night; now she's only half conscious."

"And what did the doctor say?"
"The doctor said the illness has not yet taken shape..."

12th March

I cannot continue in the way I began, dear friend: it costs me too great an effort and reopens my wounds too painfully. The illness, to use the words of the doctor, took shape, and Vera died of that illness. She did not live even two weeks after the fateful day of our fleeting tryst. I saw her once more before her death. I have no memory more cruel. I already knew from the doctor that there was no hope. Late one evening, when everyone in the house had already gone to bed, I stole up to the doors of her bedroom and glanced in. Vera lay on the bed with her eyes closed, thin, small, with a feverish flush on her cheeks. As if turned to stone I looked at her. Suddenly she opened her eyes wide, turned them on me, peered, and, reaching out an emaciated arm, pronounced:

> "What ever does he want in this sanctified place?
> That man... him there..."*

– pronounced it in a voice so terrible that I fled headlong. Almost throughout her illness she raved about *Faust* and her mother, whom she sometimes called Martha, sometimes Gretchen's mother.

Vera died. I was at her funeral. Since then I have abandoned everything and settled here for good.

Now think about what I have told you; think about her, about this creature who perished so soon. How it happened, how to interpret this incomprehensible interference of the dead in the affairs of the living, I do not know and shall never know; but you must agree that it was not a fit of capricious depression, as you put it, that made me withdraw from society. I have become a different man from the one you knew: I believe many things now that I did not believe before. All this time I have thought so much about that unfortunate woman (I almost said "girl"), about her parentage, about the secret game of fate on which we, the blind, bestow the name of blind chance. Who knows how many seeds each person living on the earth leaves, which are fated to spring up only after his death? Who can say by what mysterious chain the fate of a man is linked with the fate of his children, his descendants, and how his aspirations affect them, how his mistakes are answered for by them? We must all submit and bow our heads before the Unknown.

Yes, Vera perished, while I survived. I remember, when I was still a child, we had in the house a beautiful vase of transparent alabaster. Not a single spot defiled its virginal whiteness. One day, left on my own, I began rocking the pedestal on which it stood... the vase suddenly fell and was smashed to pieces. I froze in fright and stood motionless before the fragments. My father came in, saw me and said: "Now look what you've done: we won't have our beautiful vase any more; there's nothing that can put it right now." I began to sob. It seemed to me that I had committed a crime.

I grew up – and thoughtlessly broke a vessel a thousand times more precious...

I tell myself in vain that I could not have expected so instantaneous a denouement, that I was shocked myself by its suddenness, that I did not suspect what sort of creature Vera was. She really did know how to remain silent until the last moment. I should have fled as soon as I felt that I loved her, loved a married woman, but I stayed – and a beautiful creation was smashed to pieces, and in dumb despair do I gaze upon my handiwork.

Yes, Yeltsova guarded her daughter jealously. She protected her to the end and, at the first incautious step, carried her off with her to the grave.

It's time to close... I haven't told you even a hundredth part of what I ought, but even that has been enough for me. So let all that has risen to the surface sink again to the bottom of my soul... In closing, I will say to you that I have borne one conviction out of the experience of recent years: life is not a joke, nor an amusement, life is not even a pleasure... life is hard labour. Renunciation, constant renunciation – that is its secret meaning, its solution, not the fulfilment of cherished ideas and dreams, no matter how exalted they might be: the fulfilment of his duty, that is what a man ought to concern himself with; unless he has put chains upon himself, the iron chains of duty, he cannot reach the end of his life's journey without falling; whereas in our youth we think: the freer, the better – the further you'll go. Youth can be permitted to think that way; but it is shameful to cheer yourself with a deceit when the stern face of truth has finally looked you in the eye.

Goodbye! Previously I would have added: be happy; now I shall say to you: try to live, it is not as easy as it seems. Remember me, not in times of sadness, but in times of reflection, and preserve in your soul the image of Vera in all its untainted purity... Once again, goodbye!

Your P.B.

Yakov Pasynkov

I

It was in St Petersburg, in winter, on the first day of Shrovetide. I was invited home for lunch by one of my fellow pupils from boarding school who had had a reputation when young for being a shrinking violet, but who had turned out subsequently to be a man by no means shy. He is already dead now, like the majority of my fellows. Besides me, a certain Konstantin Alexandrovich Asanov had promised to come to lunch, and also a literary celebrity of the time. The literary celebrity kept us waiting, then finally sent a note to say that he would not be coming, and there appeared in his place a little fair-haired gentleman, one of those eternal uninvited guests in which St Petersburg so abounds.

The lunch carried on for a long time; our host did not begrudge the wines, and little by little our heads became heated. Everything that each of us hid in his soul – and who does not hide something in his soul? – came to the surface. The host's face suddenly lost its bashful and reserved expression; his eyes began to shine insolently, and his lips twisted in a vulgar grin; the fair-haired gentleman laughed in what was a rather nasty way, with a silly squealing; but Asanov surprised me most of all. This man had always been noted for his sense of decorum, but now he suddenly began rubbing his forehead, putting on airs, boasting of his connections, and constantly referring to some uncle of his, a very important person... I simply couldn't recognize him; he was blatantly mocking us... and all but turning his nose up at our company. Asanov's insolence made me angry.

"Listen," I said to him, "if we're such nonentities in your eyes, go and see your eminent uncle. But perhaps he won't let you in?"

Asanov made no reply to me, and continued rubbing his forehead.

"And who are these people?" he said again. "I mean, they don't mix in any respectable society, they're not acquainted with a single respectable woman, whereas I," he exclaimed, adroitly pulling his wallet out from a side pocket and slapping his hand against it, "have here a whole bundle of letters from a girl whose like you won't find anywhere in the world!"

Our host and the fair-haired gentleman paid no attention to Asanov's last words – they were holding on to one another's buttons and telling some kind of story – but I pricked up my ears.

"Now that's one boast too many, mister eminent-man's-nephew!" I said, moving up close to Asanov. "You don't have any letters."

"You think not?" he retorted, giving me a haughty look. "Well what's this?" He opened up his wallet and showed me ten or so letters addressed in his name... "I know that handwriting!" I thought.

I feel a flush of shame rising to my cheeks... this is most distressing for my self-esteem... Who admits willingly to an ignoble act?... But there is nothing for it, I knew in advance when I began my story that I would have to blush to the roots. And so I must reluctantly admit that...

The thing is this: Asanov had carelessly tossed the letters onto the tablecloth, awash with champagne (there was a good deal of noise in my own head too), and I exploited his inebriation to run quickly through one of those letters...

My heart contracted... Alas! I was myself in love with the girl who had been writing to Asanov, and now I could no longer be in any doubt that she loved him. All the letters, written in French, breathed tenderness and devotion...

"*Mon cher ami Constantin!*"* was how it began... and it ended with the words: "Be cautious as before, and I shall be yours or no one's."

Stunned, as if by a thunderbolt, I sat motionless for some moments, but finally came to my senses, leapt up and rushed out of the room…

A quarter of an hour later I was already in my apartment.

The Zlotnitsky family was one of the first with which I became acquainted after my move to St Petersburg from Moscow. It consisted of the father, the mother, two daughters and a son. The father, formerly a military man, already grey-haired but still well-preserved, held quite an important post, was to be found at work in the morning, slept after lunch, and in the evening played cards at his club… He was rarely at home, spoke little and unwillingly, looked out from under his brows either sullenly or indifferently, and, apart from travel-writing and geography, read nothing, but when taken ill would colour in pictures, locked up in his study, or tease the old grey parrot, Polly. His wife, a sick, consumptive woman with black, sunken eyes and a sharp nose, did not rise from the sofa for days on end, and was forever embroidering cushions; so far as I could tell, she was rather afraid of her husband, as if she had somehow been at fault before him at some time. The elder daughter, Varvara, a plump, rosy girl of about eighteen with light-brown hair, was forever sitting by the window, scrutinizing passers-by. The young son was being educated at a state-run institution, appeared at home only on Sundays, and did not like wasting words either; even the younger daughter, Sofia, the very girl with whom I had fallen in love, was of a taciturn nature. Silence reigned constantly in the Zlotnitskys' house; it was broken only by Polly's piercing cries; but guests soon got used to them and then once more experienced the weight and oppression of the eternal silence. But guests rarely dropped in on the Zlotnitskys: theirs was a dull house. The very furniture, the red-and-yellow patterned wallpaper in the drawing room, the many wicker chairs in the dining-room, the faded worsted cushions scattered on the sofas with their images of girls and dogs, the horned lamps and the gloomy portraits on the walls, it all inspired an involuntary depression, there was an air of something cold and sour about everything. When I arrived in St Petersburg I considered it my duty to present myself to the Zlotnitskys: they were related to my mother. I had difficulty sitting through an hour, and did not return for a long time; but I gradually began to go more and more often. I was attracted by Sofia, whom at first I did not like but with whom, in the end, I fell in love.

She was a girl of no great height, slim, almost thin, with a pale face, thick black hair and large, brown eyes that were always half closed. Her features, severe and abrupt, especially her compressed lips, expressed firmness and strength of will. She was known in the household as a girl with character... "She takes after the eldest sister, after Katerina," said Mrs Zlotnitskaya one day, when sitting alone with me (in her husband's presence she did not dare to mention this Katerina). "You don't know her: she's in the Caucasus, married. At the age of thirteen, imagine it, she fell in love with her present husband and announced to us there and then that she wouldn't marry another. No matter what we did – nothing was of any use! She waited till she was twenty-three, incensed her father, and in the end went and married her idol. We've not got long to wait for something of the sort with Sonyechka! May the Lord preserve her from such obstinacy! But I'm afraid for her: she's only just turned sixteen, you know, and already you can't force her to do anything..."

In came Mr Zlotnitsky; his wife fell silent straight away.

It was not with her strength of will that Sofia caught my personal fancy – no, for all her dryness, for all her lack of vivacity and imagination, she did have a sort of charm, the charm of directness, honest sincerity and spiritual purity. I respected her just as much as I loved her... It seemed to me that she was also well disposed towards me; to become disenchanted with her attachment, to become convinced of her love for another was painful for me.

The unexpected discovery I had made surprised me all the more as Mr Asanov visited the Zlotnitskys' house infrequently, much more rarely than I, and showed Sonyechka no particular favour. He was a handsome, brown-haired man with expressive, albeit rather heavy features, with shining, prominent eyes, a large, white forehead and plump little red lips beneath a thin moustache. He conducted himself extremely modestly but firmly, spoke and made judgements self-confidently, kept silent with dignity. It was evident that he thought a lot of himself. Asanov laughed rarely and even then through his teeth, and he never danced. He was of quite clumsy build. He had once served in the —— Regiment and was reputed to be an efficient officer.

"It's a strange thing!" I reflected, lying on my sofa. "How is it that I noticed nothing?..." "Be cautious as before": those words from Sofia's letter suddenly came to mind. "Ah!" I thought. "That's the way it is! See what a sly young miss! And I thought her frank and sincere... Well, just wait a little, I'll show you..."

But at that point, so far as I can recall, I began to cry bitterly and could not get to sleep all night.

The next day, some time after one o'clock, I set off for the Zlotnitskys'. The old man was out, and his wife was not sitting in her usual place: after eating some pancakes she had developed a headache and had gone to her bedroom to lie down. Varvara was standing with her shoulder leant against the window and looking into the street; Sofia was walking back and forth across the room with her arms folded across her breast; Polly was making a row.

"Ah, hello!" said Varvara indolently, as soon as I entered the room, and immediately added in a low voice: "And there goes a man with a tray on his head..." (She was in the habit of making occasional comments, as though to herself, about passers-by.)

"Hello," I replied, "hello, Sofia Nikolayevna. And where's Tatyana Vasilyevna?"

"She's gone for a rest," said Sofia, continuing to walk around the room.

"We had pancakes," remarked Varvara, without turning round. "Why didn't you come?... Where's that clerk going?"

"I didn't have the time." ("Pre-sent arms!" cried the parrot sharply.) "What a row that Polly of yours is making today!"

"He's always making a row like that," said Sofia.

We were all silent for a moment.

"He's going through the gate," said Varvara, then suddenly got up onto the window sill and opened the pane at the top.

"What's the matter?" asked Sofia.

"A beggar," replied Varvara, and she bent down, picked up from the window-sill a copper five-copeck coin, on which a grey pile of ash from a smoking candle was still heaped, threw the coin into the street, slammed the window shut, and jumped down heavily onto the floor...

"I had a very nice time yesterday," I began, sitting down in an armchair. "I had lunch with a friend; Konstantin Alexandrych was there..." (I looked at Sofia, but her brow did not even wrinkle.) "And I must confess," I continued, "we had a real binge: drank about eight bottles between the four of us."

"Really?" pronounced Sofia calmly, and shook her head.

"Yes," I continued, slightly irritated by her indifference, "and do you know, Sofia Nikolayevna, it really is true, not for nothing does the saying go: 'the truth is in wine'."

"Why's that?"

"Konstantin Alexandrych made us laugh. Just imagine: he suddenly started rubbing his forehead like this and repeating: 'What a good boy am I! I've got an eminent uncle!...'"

"Ha-ha!" rang out Varvara's brief, abrupt laugh... "Polly! Polly! Polly!" the parrot drummed out in response.

Sofia stopped in front of me and looked me in the face.

"And what did you say," she asked, "do you remember?"

I involuntarily blushed.

"I don't! I expect I was a fine one too. It really is," I added, with a significant pause, "dangerous drinking wine: you go and let out a secret and say things that nobody should know. You regret it later on, but it's already too late."

"And did you let out a secret?" asked Sofia.

"I'm not talking about myself."

Sofia turned away and again began walking around the room. I watched her, inwardly raging. "Just look at that," I thought, "a child, a baby, but what self-control she has! Simply made of stone. But just wait..."

"Sofia Nikolayevna," I said, loudly.

Sofia stopped.

"What do you want?"

"Won't you play something on the piano? By the way, I need to tell you something," I added in a lower voice.

Without saying a word, Sofia went into the reception hall; I followed her. She stopped by the piano.

"What shall I play for you?" she asked.

"Whatever you like... a Chopin nocturne."

Sofia began a nocturne. She played quite badly, but with feeling. Her sister played nothing but polkas and waltzes, and those but rarely. She would go up to the piano in her indolent way, sit down, let her burnous slip from her shoulders to her elbows (I never saw her without a burnous), begin playing a loud polka, not finish it, start on another, then suddenly sigh, get up and set off back to the window. A strange creature was that Varvara!

I sat down beside Sofia.

"Sofia Nikolayevna," I began, casting intent looks at her from the side, "I must inform you of a certain piece of news that is unpleasant for me."

"News? What news?"

"This is what... Until now I was mistaken about you, completely mistaken."

"In what way was that?" she said, continuing to play and with her eyes fixed on her fingers.

"I thought you were frank; I didn't think you knew how to be sly, conceal your feelings, be cunning…"

Sofia moved her face closer to her music.

"I don't understand you."

"And the main thing," I continued, "is that I couldn't possibly have imagined that you already knew at your age how to act out a role so skilfully."

Sofia's hands began to tremble slightly above the keys.

"What is it you're saying?" she said, still without looking at me. "I'm acting out a role?"

"Yes, you." (She smiled… I was gripped by anger…) "You pretend to be indifferent to a certain person and… and you're writing him letters," I added in a whisper.

Sofia's cheeks paled, but she did not turn towards me; she played the nocturne through to the end, rose and closed the lid of the piano.

"Where are you going?" I asked her, not without embarrassment. "Aren't you going to answer me?"

"How am I to answer you? I don't know what you're talking about… And I don't know how to pretend."

She began putting the music away…

The blood rushed to my head.

"Yes, you do know what I'm talking about," I said, standing up too, "and if you like, I'll remind you now of some of your expressions in a certain letter: 'be cautious as before'…"

Sofia gave a slight start.

"I never expected this from you," she said finally.

"And I never expected," I rejoined, "that you, you, Sofia Nikolayevna, would have favoured with your attention a man who…"

Sofia turned quickly towards me; I involuntarily backed away from her: her eyes, always half-closed, had widened to such an extent that they seemed huge, and they were flashing furiously from beneath her brows.

"Ah! If that's the way it is," she said, "then know that I love that man and that it's all one to me what opinion you hold of him and of my love for him. And what gave you the idea?... What right do you have to say that? And if I've made up my mind to do something..."

She fell silent and hurriedly left the room.

I remained. I suddenly felt so awkward and so ashamed that I hid my face in my hands. I understood all the impropriety, all the meanness of my behaviour, and, choking with shame and remorse, I stood as if in disgrace. "My God," I thought, "what have I done!"

"Anton Nikitich," came the voice of a maid from the hallway, "would you bring a glass of water quickly for Sofia Nikolayevna."

"What is it?" answered the pantryman.

"She seems to be crying..."

I shuddered and went into the drawing room for my hat.

"What were you and Sonyechka talking about?" Varvara asked me indifferently, then, after a short silence, added in a low voice: "There goes that clerk again."

I started to take my leave.

"But where are you going? Wait: Mummy will be out in a minute."

"No, I really can't," I said, "better another time."

At that moment, to my horror, and I mean horror, Sofia stepped firmly into the drawing room. Her face was paler than normal, and her eyelids were just a little red. She did not even glance at me.

"Look, Sonya," said Varvara, "some clerk keeps walking about outside our house."

"Some sort of spy..." remarked Sofia, coldly and scornfully.

This was simply too much! I left and really cannot remember how I dragged myself home.

* * *

I was quite wretched, so wretched and bitter that it cannot even be described. In the space of twenty-four hours, two such cruel blows! I had learnt that Sofia loved another and I had lost her respect for ever. I felt crushed and shamed to such an extent that I could not even be indignant with myself. Lying on the sofa and with my face turned towards the wall, I was giving myself up with a kind of fervent enjoyment to the first waves of despairing anguish, when suddenly I heard footsteps in the room. I raised my head and saw one of my closest friends – Yakov Pasynkov.

I was prepared to be angry with anyone who might enter my room that day, but I could never be angry with Pasynkov; on the contrary, despite the grief that was devouring me, I was inwardly pleased at his arrival and nodded to him. He, as usual, walked around the room a couple of times, grunting and stretching his long limbs, stood in front of me for a while in silence and then sat down in silence in the corner.

I had known Pasynkov for a very long time, almost since childhood. He was educated in that same private boarding school run by Winterkeller, the German, in which I too spent three years. Yakov's father, a poor retired major, a most honest man, but somewhat unsound in mind, brought him to this German as a seven-year-old boy, paid for him for a year in advance, left Moscow, and proceeded to disappear without trace... Occasionally there were dark, strange rumours about him. Only some eight years later was it reliably learned that he had drowned in spring high water while crossing the River Irtysh. What had taken him to Siberia – the Lord knows. Yakov had no other relatives; his mother had died long before. And so he was left on Winterkeller's hands. True, Yakov did have one distant relation, an aunt, but one so poor that she was at first afraid to visit her nephew in case she was saddled with him. Her fear proved unfounded: the kind-hearted German kept Yakov with him, allowed him to study along with the other pupils, fed him (although at table he was not served dessert on weekdays) and had his clothes made out of the worn camlet housecoats (tobacco-coloured, for the most part) of his own mother, an extremely aged but still very spirited and efficient Lithuanian. In consequence of all these circumstances, and in consequence of Yakov's subordinate position in the boarding school generally, his fellows were offhand with him, regarded him superciliously and sometimes called him "the woman's housecoat", sometimes "the bonnet's nephew" (his aunt constantly wore the strangest bonnet with a bunch of yellow ribbons sticking up in the shape of an artichoke), sometimes "Yermak's son"* (since his father had drowned in the Irtysh). But in spite of these nicknames, in spite of his funny clothes and his extreme poverty, everyone was very fond of him, indeed, it was impossible not to be fond of him: there was not a kinder, nobler soul, I think, in all the world. He also did very well in his studies.

When I saw him for the first time, he was about sixteen, while I had only just turned thirteen. I was a very vain and spoilt boy, I had grown up in quite a rich household, and for that reason, when I joined the boarding school, I made haste to become good friends with a little prince, the object of Winterkeller's special attentions, and with two or three other little aristocrats, while putting on airs with all the others. I did not even favour Pasynkov with my attention. This lanky and awkward fellow wearing an ugly jacket and trousers that were too short, from beneath which there peeped thick cotton stockings, seemed to me rather like a pageboy picked from the house servants, or the son of a tradesman. Pasynkov was very polite and meek with everyone, although he never tried to ingratiate himself with anybody; if he was rejected, he did not demean himself and did not sulk, but held himself aloof, as though regretfully biding his time. And that was how he acted with me. Some two months went by. Once, on a clear summer's day, walking from the yard to the garden after a noisy game of ball, I caught sight of Pasynkov sitting on a bench under a tall lilac bush. He was reading a book. I glanced in passing at the binding, and read on the spine the name of Schiller: *Schillers Werke*. I stopped.

"Do you really know German?" I asked Pasynkov...

To this day I begin to feel ashamed when I remember how much disdain there was in the very sound of my voice... Pasynkov quietly raised his small but expressive eyes to look at me and replied, "Yes, I do; what about you?"

"I'll say!" I retorted, offended now, and I would have gone on my way, but something held me back.

"And what is it exactly you're reading by Schiller?" I asked, with my previous haughtiness.

"Now? I'm reading 'Resignation':* it's a fine poem. Would you like me to read it to you? Sit down here beside me on the bench."

I wavered a little, but sat down. Pasynkov began reading. He knew German much better than I did: he had to explain the meaning of some of the lines to me, but I was no longer ashamed either of my ignorance, or of his superiority over me. From that day, from that very reading, alone together in the garden in the shade of the lilac, I came to love Pasynkov with all my soul, became good friends with him, and subordinated myself to him completely.

I remember his appearance at that time vividly. Yet even afterwards he changed but little. He was tall, thin, lanky and rather clumsy. Narrow shoulders and a sunken chest gave him a sickly look, although he could not complain about his health. His large head, rounded towards the top, leant slightly to one side, his soft, light-brown hair hung in straggly locks around his slender neck. His face was not handsome and could even appear funny due to his long, plump and reddish nose, which seemed to overhang his wide and straight lips; but his open forehead was fine, and when he smiled, his small grey eyes shone with such meek and affectionate good nature that anyone looking at him would feel warm and cheerful at heart. I also remember his voice, soft and even, with a particularly pleasant sort of huskiness. Generally he spoke little and with noticeable difficulty; but when he became animated, his speech flowed freely and – strange to say! – his voice became still softer, it was as if his gaze retreated inwards and faded away, while the whole of his face was gently aglow. On his lips the words "goodness", "truth", "life", "learning", "love", no matter with what rapture they were pronounced, never sounded a false note. Without strain, without effort he entered the realm of the ideal; his chaste soul was ready at any time to stand before "the shrine of beauty";* it merely awaited the greeting, the touch of another soul... Pasynkov was a romantic, one of the last romantics I happened to meet. Romantics nowadays, as is well known, have almost become extinct; at least, amongst today's young people there are none. So much the worse for today's young people!

I spent about three years completely at one, as they say, with Pasynkov. I was the confidant of his first love. With what grateful attention and sympathy did I hear out his confessions! The object of his passion was Winterkeller's niece, a sweet, fair-haired little German girl, with a plump, almost childish little face and trustingly gentle pale-blue eyes. She was very kind and sentimental, liked Matthison, Uhland* and Schiller, and declaimed their poetry very pleasantly in her shy and resonant voice. Pasynkov's love was the most platonic; he saw his beloved only on Sundays (she came to play forfeits with Winterkeller's children) and had little conversation with her; but once, when she said to him "*mein lieber, lieber Herr Jacob*",* he could not get to sleep all night for an excess of well-being. It did not even occur to him then that she said "*mein lieber*" to all his fellows. I also remember his grief and melancholy when the news suddenly spread that Fraulein Friederiche (that was her name) was going to marry Herr Knifftus, the owner of a prospering butcher's shop, a very handsome and even educated man, and was marrying not out of obedience to parental will alone, but also for love. Pasynkov was very wretched then, and he suffered particularly on the day of the young couple's first visit. The former Fräulein, but now already Frau Friederiche, presented him once more by the name of "*lieber Herr Jacob*" to her husband, everything about whom was shining: his eyes, his black hair curled up into a quiff, his forehead, his teeth, the buttons on his tailcoat, the chain on his waistcoat, and the very boots on his, incidentally rather large, splay-toed feet. Pasynkov shook Mr Knifftus by the hand and wished him (and wished him sincerely too – of that I am certain) complete and long-lasting happiness. This took place in my presence. I remember with what surprise and sympathy I gazed then at Yakov. He seemed a hero to me!... And afterwards what sad conversations there were between us! "Seek solace in art," I said to him. "Yes," he answered me, "and in poetry." "And in friendship," I added. "And in friendship," he repeated. Oh, happy days!...

It was sad for me to part with Pasynkov! Just before I left, he had finally, after a long period of effort and trouble, and after correspondence that was often amusing, got hold of his papers and entered the university. He continued to live at Winterkeller's expense, but instead of camlet jackets and trousers he now received normal clothing in reward for the lessons on various subjects that he gave to the younger pupils. Pasynkov never changed the way he treated me right up until the end of my stay at the boarding school, although the difference in age between us was already beginning to tell and, as I recall, I was starting to be jealous of him in relation to some of his new fellow students. His influence on me was most salutary. Unfortunately, it did not last long. I shall give just one example. As a child I had acquired the habit of lying... I could not bring myself to tell a lie in front of Yakov. But it was a particular joy for me to go for a walk alone with him or to pace up and down the room beside him as, without a glance at me, he recited poetry in his soft and focused voice. It truly seemed to me then that he and I were slowly, little by little, becoming detached from the earth and carried away somewhere, to some radiant, mysterious wonderland... I remember one night. He and I were sitting under that same lilac bush: we had come to love that spot. All our fellows were already asleep, but we had got up quietly, fumbled our way into our clothes in the darkness and stolen out "to dream a little". It was quite warm outside, but a fresh breeze blew at times and made us huddle up still closer to one another. We talked, we talked a great deal and with fervour, so that we even interrupted each other, although we did not argue. Countless stars shone in the sky. Yakov raised his eyes and, gripping my hand, exclaimed softly:

> Above us
> Heaven and the stars eternal…
> And then above the stars their Maker…*

A reverential tremor ran through me; I turned quite cold and fell onto his shoulder… My heart was overflowing…

Where are those raptures now? Alas, where youth is too!

I met Yakov in St Petersburg some eight years later. I had just joined the civil service and somebody had got him a position in some government department. Our meeting was the most joyous. I shall never forget the moment when, sitting at home one day, I suddenly heard his voice in the entrance hall… How I jumped, with what a beating heart did I leap up and throw myself upon his neck, without giving him the time to take off his fur coat and unwind his scarf! How greedily I gazed at him through involuntary, bright tears of emotion! He had aged a little in the previous seven years; wrinkles, fine as the trace of a needle, furrowed his brow here and there, his cheeks had sunk slightly, and his hair was thinner, but there was almost no more growth of beard and his smile remained the same; and his laughter, the dear, inner, seemingly breathless laughter, remained the same…

My God! What, oh what, did we not talk over that day!… How many favourite poems did we recite to one another! I started to try and persuade him to move in with me, but he would not agree to it; yet he did promise to drop in on me daily, and he kept his promise.

And Pasynkov had not changed in spirit. He stood before me, the same romantic as I had known him. No matter how the coldness of life, the bitter cold of experience gripped him, the tender flower that had bloomed early in the heart of my friend survived in all its untouched beauty. He showed no sign even of sadness, even of pensiveness: he was quiet as before, but ever cheerful in spirit.

In St Petersburg he lived as if in a wilderness, not reflecting on the future and hardly associating with anyone. I introduced him to the Zlotnitskys. He called on them quite often. While not proud, he was not shy either, but even with them, as everywhere, he said little; yet still they came to like him. Even the difficult old man, Tatyana Vasilyevna's husband, treated him affectionately, and both of the taciturn girls quickly got used to him.

Sometimes he would arrive, bringing with him in the back pocket of his frock coat some newly published work, and would hesitate for a long time about reading it, would keep stretching his neck out to one side, like a bird, looking to check whether he could; finally he would find a space in a corner (he liked sitting in corners generally), get the book out and start to read, at first in a whisper, then louder and louder, occasionally breaking in on himself with brief judgements or exclamations. I noticed that Varvara sat down with him and listened to him more readily than her sister, although, of course, she understood him but little: literature did not interest her. She would sometimes sit in front of Pasynkov with her chin resting on her hands, gazing not into his eyes, but generally into his face as a whole, and would not utter a word, but only heave a sudden loud sigh. In the evenings we played forfeits, especially on Sundays and on holidays. Then we were joined by two young ladies, sisters, distant relations of the Zlotnitskys, small, rotund, and dreadful gigglers, and by several cadets and officer cadets, very kind, quiet boys. Pasynkov always sat beside

Tatyana Vasilyevna, and together they thought up what had to be done by the person whose turn it was.

Sofia did not like the displays of affection and kisses with which forfeits are generally paid, while Varvara would be annoyed when she had to try to find or guess anything. The young ladies giggled away unconcerned – where did they get the laughter from? – and sometimes, looking at them, I would be gripped by annoyance, but Pasynkov only smiled and shook his head. Old man Zlotnitsky did not get involved in our games and even looked at us not entirely kindly from behind the doors of his study. Only once, quite unexpectedly, did he come out to us and suggest that the person whose turn it was should dance a waltz with him; it goes without saying that we agreed. The forfeit was Tatyana Vasilyevna's: she turned quite red, became embarrassed and ashamed like a girl of fifteen – but her husband immediately ordered Sofia to sit down at the piano, he went up to his wife and made two circuits with her, in the old-fashioned way, in triple time. I remember how his face, bilious and dark, with unsmiling eyes, now appeared, now disappeared, turning slowly with no alteration of its stern expression. He took long steps and bobbed up and down while waltzing, whereas his wife took quick little steps and pressed her face against his chest as though in fear. He led her to her seat, bowed to her, went off to his room and closed the door. Sofia tried to get up. But Varvara asked her to continue the waltz, went up to Pasynkov and, reaching out her hand, said with an awkward smile: "Will you?" Pasynkov was surprised, yet leapt up – he was always known for his refined good manners – and took Varvara by the waist, but slipped at the very first step and, quickly detaching himself from his lady, rolled straight into the cupboard on which stood the parrot's cage... The cage fell off, the parrot took fright and cried out: "Pre-sent arms!" General laughter broke out... Zlotnitsky appeared on the threshold of his study, gave a stern glance and slammed the door. From that time on one only had to recall this occurrence in Varvara's presence for her to start laughing at once and look at Pasynkov with such an expression as if anything cleverer than what he had done then would be impossible to imagine.

Pasynkov was very fond of music. He often asked Sofia to play him something, and would sit to one side and listen, occasionally joining in with his thin voice on sentimental notes. He particularly liked Schubert's 'The Stars'.* He claimed that when 'The Stars' was played in his presence, it always seemed to him that along with the sounds some long blue rays poured directly into his breast from on high. To this day, at the sight of a cloudless night sky with gently shifting stars, I still always remember Schubert's melody and Pasynkov... A certain trip out of town also comes to mind. A whole group of us drove in two hired four-seater carriages to Pargolovo. I seem to recall the carriages being taken from Vladimirskaya Street; they were very old, light-blue in colour, on round springs, with wide boxes and wisps of hay inside; the jaded brown horses carried us along at a lumbering trot, each limping on a different leg. We spent a long time strolling through the pine woods around Pargolovo, drank milk from earthenware jugs, and ate wild strawberries with sugar. The weather was wonderful. Varvara did not like to walk a great deal, as she soon became exhausted, but on this occasion she did not lag behind us. She took off her hat, her hair came loose, her heavy features became animated and her cheeks turned red. On meeting two peasant girls in the wood, she suddenly seated herself on the ground, called them over, and although she did not say anything nice to them, sat them down beside her. Sofia looked at them from a distance with a cold smile and did not approach them. She was walking with Asanov, but Zlotnitsky remarked that Varvara was a real mother hen. Varvara stood up and walked away. She went up to Pasynkov several times during the trip and said to him: "Yakov Ivanych, I want to tell you something" – but what she wanted to tell him remained unknown.

However, it is time I returned to my story.

* * *

I was pleased that Pasynkov had come; but when I remembered what I had done the day before, I became inexpressibly ashamed, and I hurriedly turned back to the wall again. After a little while Yakov asked me if I was well.

"Yes," I replied, through gritted teeth, "only I've got a headache."

Yakov made no reply and picked up a book. More than an hour passed; I already meant to confess everything to Yakov... when suddenly the bell rang in the entrance hall.

The door onto the staircase was opened... I listened intently... Asanov was asking my man if I was at home.

Pasynkov stood up; he did not like Asanov and, whispering to me that he would go and have a lie-down on my bed, he set off into my bedroom.

A minute later, in came Asanov.

From his flushed face alone and from his perfunctory and dry bow I guessed that he had come to see me not without good reason. "What's it going to be?" I thought.

"My dear sir," he began, sitting down quickly in an armchair, "I've come to see you so that you might resolve a certain doubt for me."

"Namely?"

"Namely: I wish to know whether you are a man of honour."

I flared up.

"What does that mean?" I asked.

"This is what it means..." he said, as though hammering out every word, "yesterday I showed you a wallet of letters to me from a certain person... Today you repeated to that person with reproach – with reproach, note – several expressions from those letters, having not the least right to do so. I wish to know how you explain this?"

"And I wish to know what right *you* have to question me?" I replied, trembling all over from fury and inner shame. "It was your own choice to show off about your uncle, your correspondence; what have I got to do with it? All your letters are intact, aren't they?"

"The letters are intact; but I was in such a state yesterday that you could easily have..."

"In short, my dear sir," I began, intentionally speaking as loudly as possible, "please leave me in peace, do you hear? I want to hear nothing more, and I don't intend explaining anything to you. Go and ask that person for explanations!" (I felt that my head was beginning to spin.)

Asanov directed at me a gaze to which he evidently sought to lend an expression of mocking shrewdness, plucked at his moustache and rose unhurriedly.

"Now I know what to think," he said, "your face gives you away more than anything. But I should point out to you that honourable people don't behave like this... To read a letter by stealth and then go bothering an honourable girl..."

"Go to the devil!" I shouted, stamping my feet. "And send me your second; I don't intend speaking to you."

"Please don't lecture me," said Asanov coldly, "and I was intending to send you my second already."

He left. I fell onto the sofa and hid my face in my hands. Somebody touched me on the shoulder; I took my hands away – before me stood Pasynkov.

"What's this? Is it true?" he asked me. "Did you read another person's letter?"

I did not have the strength to answer him, but gave my head an affirmative nod.

Pasynkov went up to the window and, standing with his back to me, said: "You read a girl's letter to Asanov. Who was this girl, then?"

"Sofia Zlotnitskaya," I replied, in the way an accused man answers a judge.

For a long time Pasynkov did not utter a word.

"Only passion can to a certain extent excuse you," he began at last. "So are you in love with Zlotnitskaya?"

"Yes."

Pasynkov was again silent for a moment.

"I thought so. And today you went to see her and began reproaching her..."

"Yes, yes, yes..." I said despairingly. "Now you can despise me..."

Pasynkov passed up and down the room a couple of times.

"And does she love him?" he asked.

"She does..."

Pasynkov lowered his head and gazed motionless for a long time at the floor.

"Well, this needs to be helped along," he began, raising his head, "it can't be left like this."

And he picked up his hat.

"And where are you going?"

"To see Asanov."

I leapt up from the sofa.

"But I won't let you. For pity's sake! How can you? What will he think?"

Pasynkov looked at me.

"So do you really think it's better to set this silliness in motion, destroy yourself and have a young girl disgraced?"

"But what will you say to Asanov?"

"I'll try to make him see sense, I'll say that you ask his forgiveness..."

"But I don't want to apologize to him!"

"You don't want to? Are you not at fault then?"

I looked at Pasynkov: I was struck by his calm and stern, albeit sad expression; it was new to me. I made no reply and sat down on the sofa.

Pasynkov went out.

With what terrible anguish did I await his return! With what cruel slowness did the time pass! Finally he came back – it was late.

"Well?" I asked in a timid voice.

"Thank God!" he replied. "Everything's settled."

"You've been to Asanov's?"

"Yes."

"What was he like? Difficult, I expect?" I said with an effort.

"No, I couldn't say that. I expected worse... He... he's not such a boorish man as I thought he was."

"Well, and other than him, you've not called on anyone?" I asked after a slight pause.

"I called on the Zlotnitskys."

"Ah!..." (My heart began beating hard. I did not dare look Pasynkov in the eye.) "How is she?"

"Sofia Nikolayevna is a good, sensible girl... Yes, she's a good girl. At first she felt awkward, but then she relaxed. Still, our entire conversation lasted no more than five minutes."

"And you... told her everything... about me... everything?"

"I told her what was necessary."

"I won't be able to go and visit them any more now!" I said mournfully...

"Why's that, then? No, you can, occasionally. On the contrary, you ought to go and see them without fail, so that nobody gets any ideas..."

"Oh, Yakov, you're going to despise me now!" I exclaimed, scarcely holding back my tears.

"Me? Despise you?..." (His affectionate eyes lit up with love.) "Despise you... silly man! Have you had it easy, then? Aren't you suffering?"

He reached out his hand to me, I threw myself onto his neck, and burst into sobs.

After a few days, in the course of which I could see that Pasynkov was very much out of sorts, I resolved at last to call on the Zlotnitskys. What I felt as I stepped into their drawing room is difficult to convey in words; I remember that I could hardly make out anybody's face and my voice broke in my chest. And it was no easier for Sofia: she was visibly forcing herself to enter into conversation with me, but her eyes avoided mine just as mine did hers, and in every one of her movements, in the whole of her being, could be discerned constraint mixed with – why hide the truth? – with secret loathing. I sought to relieve both her and myself of such distressing sensations as quickly as possible. This meeting was, fortunately, the last… before her marriage. A sudden change in my fate drew me away to the other end of Russia, and it was for a long time that I said goodbye to St Petersburg, the Zlotnitsky family and, what was for me most painful of all, to good Yakov Pasynkov.

2

SOME SEVEN YEARS PASSED. I do not consider it necessary to relate precisely what happened to me during all that time. How I did roam across Russia, though, paying visits to the back of beyond, and thank God too! The back of beyond is not so terrible as some people think, and in the best-hidden spots of dense forest, beneath fallen trees and brushwood, there grow fragrant flowers.

One day in spring, while travelling on official business through a small district town in one of the distant provinces in the east of Russia, through the dull window of my tarantass I caught sight of a man in front of a shop on the square, whose face seemed to me extremely familiar. I looked closely at this man and, to my no small delight, recognized in him Yelisei, Pasynkov's servant.

I immediately ordered the coachman to stop, leapt out of the tarantass and went up to Yelisei.

"Hello, my friend!" I said, concealing my excitement with difficulty. "Are you here with your master?"

"With my master," he said slowly, then suddenly exclaimed: "Ah, is it you, sir? I didn't even recognize you!"

"Are you here with Yakov Ivanych?"

"With him, sir, with him... Who else would I be with?"

"Take me to him quickly."

"As you say, as you say! This way, if you please, this way... We've put up here at the inn."

And Yelisei led me across the square, constantly repeating: "Well now, how pleased Yakov Ivanych will be!"

This Yelisei, a man of Kalmyk origins, was extremely ugly and even savage to look at, but he was most kind-hearted and not stupid, he loved Pasynkov passionately, and had served him for about ten years.

"How's Yakov Ivanych's health?" I asked him.

Yelisei turned his small, dark-yellow face towards me.

"Ah, it's bad, sir… it's bad, sir! You won't recognize him… It doesn't look as if he's got long left to live in this world. That's the reason why we're stuck here, otherwise we were travelling to Odessa, you know, to get treatment."

"And where are you travelling from?"

"From Siberia, sir."

"Siberia?"

"That's right, sir. Yakov Ivanych was working there, sir. That's where he got his wound, sir."

"Has he joined the military, then?"

"Oh no, sir. He was in the civil service, sir."

"What strange goings-on!" I thought. Meanwhile we had come close to the inn, and Yelisei ran on ahead to announce me. In the first years of our separation Pasynkov and I had corresponded quite frequently, but I had received his last letter some four years earlier and knew nothing of him since then.

"This way please, sir, this way please!" Yelisei called to me from the stairs. "Yakov Ivanych very much wants to see you, sir."

I hurriedly ran up the shaky steps, went into a small, dark room – and I was heart-stricken… On a narrow bed, underneath his greatcoat, as pale as a dead man, lay Pasynkov, reaching out to me a bare, emaciated arm. I rushed to him and hugged him convulsively.

"Yasha!" I exclaimed at last. "What's the matter with you?"

"Nothing," he replied in a weak voice, "just a little under the weather. What chance brought you here?"

I sat down on the chair beside Pasynkov's bed and, without letting his hands out of mine, I began looking into his face. I recognized the features dear to me: the expression of his eyes and his smile had not changed; but what had illness done to him!

He noticed the impression he had made on me.

"I've not shaved for two or three days," he said, "well, and my hair's not combed either; otherwise I'm... still not so bad."

"Please, Yasha, tell me," I began, "what's this that Yelisei's told me?... Are you wounded?"

"Oh! That's a long story," he said. "I'll tell you later. It's quite true, I've been wounded, and just imagine, what did it? An arrow."

"An arrow?"

"Yes, an arrow, only not a mythological one, not Cupid's dart, but a real arrow of some very flexible wood, with an expertly made point on the end... Such an arrow produces a very unpleasant sensation, especially when it hits the lungs."

"But how did it happen? For pity's sake..."

"Like this. You know there have always been a lot of funny things in my fate. Do you remember my comical correspondence on the matter of procuring my papers? And now I've been wounded in a funny way. It's true, what decent man in our enlightened century would allow himself to be wounded by an arrow? And not by accident, note, not during some games or other, but in a conflict."

"But you're still not telling me..."

"Just wait a moment," he interrupted me. "You know that soon after your departure from St Petersburg I was transferred to Novgorod. I spent quite a long while in Novgorod and, I must confess, I was bored, although I did meet with a certain creature there..." he sighed. "Still, it's not the time for that now; but about two years ago a splendid post came my way, rather far off, it's true, in the Irkutsk area, but what's wrong with that! My father and I were evidently fated to see Siberia. It's a fine country, Siberia! Rich, free and easy – anyone will tell you that. I liked it there very much. I had non-Russian people under me; a quiet lot, but to my cost they took it into their heads, about ten of them, no more, to carry some contraband. I was sent to intercept them. I intercepted them right enough, only one of them, being stupid, I suppose, decided to defend himself and went and treated me to this arrow... I almost died, but I recovered. Now here I am going to complete my treatment... My superiors – may God grant them all good health – supplied the money."

Pasynkov lowered his head onto the pillow in exhaustion and fell silent. A slight flush spread across his cheeks. He closed his eyes.

"He can't talk much," said Yelisei in a low voice – he had not left the room.

Silence fell; all that could be heard was the sick man's heavy breathing.

"And so," he continued, when he had opened his eyes once again, "here I am sitting in this rotten little town for a second week... I must have caught a cold. I'm being treated by the local district doctor – you'll see him; he seems to know his business. Anyway, I'm very pleased about this happening, otherwise how would I have met up with you?" (And he took me by the hand. His hand, only recently as cold as ice, was now on fire.) "You tell me something about yourself," he began once more, throwing his greatcoat off his chest, "after all, we last saw one another God knows when."

I made haste to carry out his wish, anything to stop him talking, and started my account. At first he listened to me with great attention, then asked for a drink, before again beginning to close his eyes and toss his head about on the pillow. I advised him to go to sleep for a while, adding that I would not be travelling on until he had recovered, and would put up in a room alongside his.

"It's very unpleasant here..." Pasynkov tried to begin, but I put my hand over his mouth, then quietly went out.

Yelisei followed me out as well.

"What is this, Yelisei? He's dying, isn't he?" I asked his faithful servant.

Yelisei just waved his hand and turned away.

After dismissing the coachman and hurriedly moving into the adjacent room, I went to see whether Pasynkov had fallen asleep. By his door I bumped into a tall man, very fat and ponderous. His face, pockmarked and flabby, expressed indolence, and nothing more; he could not keep his tiny little eyes open, and his lips shone as if he had just been asleep.

"Allow me to enquire," I asked him, "whether you are the doctor?"

The fat man looked at me, earnestly raising his beetling forehead with his eyebrows.

"Indeed I am, sir," he said at last.

"Do me a service, doctor, would you mind coming in here, into my room? Yakov Ivanych seems to be asleep now; I'm his friend and should like to have a talk with you about his illness, which worries me a great deal."

"Very well, sir," replied the doctor, with such an expression, it was as if he wished to say: "What makes you talk so much? I'd have come anyway" – and he set off after me.

"Tell me, please," I began, as soon as he had lowered himself onto a chair, "is my friend's condition dangerous? What do you find?"

"Yes," the fat man calmly replied.

"And... is it very dangerous?"

"Yes, it's dangerous."

"So that he might... even die?"

"He might."

I confess, I gave my interlocutor a look almost of hatred.

"Then for pity's sake," I began, "some measures must be resorted to, a consultation summoned or something... After all, you can't just... For pity's sake!"

"A consultation, that's possible. Why not? That's possible. Call in Ivan Yefremych..."

The doctor spoke with an effort and sighed constantly. His stomach rose noticeably when he spoke, as if pushing out every word.

"Who is Ivan Yefremych?"

"The town doctor."

"Shouldn't we send to the provincial centre – what do you think? There must be good doctors there."

"Why yes, that's possible."

"And who is considered the best doctor there?"

"The best? Kolrabus was the doctor there... only he was due to be transferred somewhere. But then to tell the truth, it really isn't necessary to send for anyone."

"Why's that?"

"Even a doctor from the provincial centre won't be any help to your friend."

"Is he really so ill?"

"Indeed he is, he's been punctured."

"So what exactly is wrong with him?"

"He's been wounded... So his lungs are damaged... well and then he's caught a cold too, developed a fever... well, and so on. And there's no reserves: without reserves, you know it yourself, a man can't manage."

We were both silent for a moment.

"We could try homeopathy, perhaps..." the fat man said, throwing me a sidelong glance.

"What do you mean, homeopathy? You're an allopath, aren't you?"

"Well, what if I am an allopath? Do you think I don't know homeopathy? As well as the next man. Our pharmacist here gives homeopathic treatment, but he doesn't even have any degree."

"Well," I thought, "things are bad!"

"No, doctor," I said, "better you treat him by your normal method."

"As you wish, sir."

The fat man stood up and sighed.

"Are you going in to him?" I asked.

"Yes, I need to have a look at him."

And he left the room.

I did not follow him: to see him at the bedside of my poor sick friend was beyond my strength. I called my man and ordered him to go immediately to the provincial centre, to ask there for the best doctor, and to be sure to bring him back. There was a knocking in the corridor; I quickly opened the door.

The doctor was already coming out of Pasynkov's room.

"Well?" I asked him in a whisper.

"Nothing really, I've prescribed a mixture."

"I've made up my mind, doctor, to send to the provincial centre. I don't doubt your skill, but you know yourself: two heads are better than one."

"Well then, that's praiseworthy!" the fat man said, and he started going downstairs. He was evidently getting tired of me.

I went into Pasynkov's room.

"Did you see the local Aesculapius?*" he asked me.

"I did," I replied.

"What I like about him," began Pasynkov, "is his astonishing calmness. A doctor ought to be a phlegmatic, didn't he? It's very encouraging for the patient."

It goes without saying that I did not think of arguing with him.

Towards the evening, contrary to my expectations, Pasynkov felt better. He asked Yelisei to set up the samovar, announced to me that he would be treating me to tea and would have a cup himself, and became noticeably more cheerful. However, I still tried not to let him talk, and, seeing that he did not want to relax at all, I asked him whether he wanted me to read him anything.

"Like at Winterkeller's, remember?" he replied. "Please do, it would be a pleasure. What shall we read then? Have a look, will you, the books are over there on my window sill..."

I went over to the window and picked up the first book that came to hand...

"What is it?" he asked.

"Lermontov."

"Ah! Lermontov! Splendid! Pushkin's greater, of course... Do you remember: 'Now once more have storm clouds gathered in the silence o'er my head...' or: 'Now for the final time I dare your sweet image in my thoughts to kiss'.* Ah, wonderful, wonderful! But Lermontov's good too. You know what, old fellow, go on and open it up at random and read!"

I opened the book and became embarrassed: I had fallen upon 'The Testament'. I was about to turn over the page, but Pasynkov noticed my movement and said hurriedly: "No, no, no, read what came up."

There was nothing for it: I read 'The Testament'.

"It's a fine thing!" said Pasynkov, as soon as I had uttered the last line. "A fine thing! But it's strange," he added after a short silence, "strange that it was 'The Testament' in particular that you came upon... Strange!"

I began to read another poem, but Pasynkov was not listening to me; he was gazing off in another direction, and another couple of times he repeated: "Strange!"

I lowered the book onto my lap.

"'There is a girl who lives nearby',"* he whispered, then, turning to me, he suddenly asked: "Well then, do you remember Sofia Zlotnitskaya?"

I blushed.

"How could I fail to remember her!"

"She got married, didn't she?"

"To Asanov, ages ago. I wrote to you about it."

"That's right, that's right, you did. Did her father forgive her in the end?"

"He did, but he wouldn't receive Asanov."

"Stubborn old man! Well, and what's the word, are they happy together?"

"I really don't know... I think they are. They live in the country in —— Province; I haven't seen them, but I've travelled past."

"And do they have children?"

"I think they do... By the way, Pasynkov?" I questioned.

He glanced towards me.

"Admit it; you didn't want to answer my question then, as I recall: you told her that I loved her, didn't you?"

"I told her everything, the whole truth... I always told her the truth. To be secretive with her – that would have been wrong!"

Pasynkov was silent for a moment.

"Well, tell me then," he began again, "did you soon stop loving her or not?"

"Not soon, but I did stop loving her. What's the use of sighing in vain?"

Pasynkov turned his face back towards me.

"Well, old fellow," he began, and his lips started to quiver, "I am no match for you: I still haven't stopped loving her."

"What!" I exclaimed in inexpressible astonishment: "So did you love her, then?"

"I did," Pasynkov pronounced slowly, and drew both hands up behind his head. "How I loved her, that God alone knows. I've told nobody about it, nobody in the world, and I intended to tell nobody... but so be it! I have not much time left, they say, to live upon this earth...* But that's all right!"

Pasynkov's unexpected confession had so surprised me that I could say absolutely nothing, and only thought: "Is it possible? How is it that I didn't suspect it?"

"Yes," he continued, as though talking to himself, "I loved her. I didn't stop loving her, even when I learnt that her heart belonged to Asanov. But it was hard for me to learn that! If she'd fallen in love with you, I would at least have been glad for you; but Asanov... What could she have liked about him? His good fortune! But betray her feeling, stop loving him, that she simply couldn't do. An honest soul doesn't change..."

I recalled Asanov's visit after the fateful lunch and Pasynkov's intervention, and I involuntarily clasped my hands together.

"You learnt it all from me, you poor fellow!" I exclaimed: "And still you took it upon yourself to go and see her then!"

"Yes," Pasynkov began again, "that conversation with her... I shall never forget it. That was when I learnt, that was when I understood the meaning of the word I had long ago picked out: *Resignation*. Yet still she remained my constant dream, my ideal... And pitiful is he who lives without an ideal!"

I gazed at Pasynkov: his eyes, which seemed to be directed into the distance, shone with a feverish lustre.

"I loved her," he continued, "I loved her, her, calm, honest, untouchable, incorruptible; when she went away, I almost went mad from grief... Since then I've loved absolutely no one..."

And suddenly, turning away, he pressed his face against the pillow and quietly began to cry.

I leapt up, bent down towards him and started to comfort him...

"It's fine," he said, raising his head a little and giving his hair a shake, "it's just that I felt a little bitter, a little sorry... for myself, that is... But it's all fine. It's all the poetry's fault. Come on, read me some more, something a bit more cheerful."

I picked up the Lermontov, started turning the pages over quickly; but, almost as if on purpose, I kept coming upon poems which might have upset Pasynkov. Finally I read him 'The Gifts of the Terek'.

"Rhetorical blather!" my poor friend pronounced in the tones of a mentor: "Yet there are some good bits. I tried to launch into poetry myself in your absence, old fellow, and started a poem called 'The Cup of Life' – nothing came of it! It's our business to empathize, old fellow, not to create... But I'm a bit tired; I'll have a little sleep – what do you think? What a splendid thing it is to sleep and dream, just think! The whole of our life is a dream and the best thing in it, again, is dreaming."*

"And poetry?" I asked.

"And poetry is a dream too, only a heavenly one."

Pasynkov closed his eyes.

I stood for a little while at his bedside. I did not think he could fall asleep quickly, yet his breathing was becoming more even and more drawn out. I left on tiptoe, returned to my room and lay down on the sofa. I thought for a long time about what Pasynkov had told me, remembered many things, marvelled, and finally fell asleep myself…

Somebody nudged me; I came to: before me stood Yelisei.

"Please come to the master," he said.

I got up straight away.

"What's the matter with him?"

"He's raving."

"Raving? Has he not been like it before?"

"He has, he was raving last night too; only today it's something awful."

I went into Pasynkov's room. He was not lying, but sitting on his bed with the whole of his trunk bent forward, quietly spreading his hands, smiling and talking, constantly talking in an inaudible and weak voice like the rustling of reeds. His eyes were wandering. The sad glow of the night light, set down on the floor and shielded with a book, was a motionless patch on the ceiling; Pasynkov's face seemed even paler in the semi-darkness.

I went up to him and called him – he did not respond. I started to listen closely to his babbling: he was raving about Siberia, about its forests. At times there was some sense in his ravings.

"What trees!" he whispered. "Right up to the sky. How much frost there is on them! Silver… Snowdrifts… And here are some little tracks… first there was a hare hopping about, then a white ermine… No, it was my father running by with my papers. There he is… There he is! Got to go; the moon's shining. Got to go and find my papers… Ah! A flower, a scarlet flower – Sofia's there… There, the little bells are ringing, then it's the frost ringing… Oh no, it's silly bullfinches hopping about in the bushes, whistling… See them, with their red breasts! It's cold… Ah! There's Asanov… Ah yes, he's a cannon, isn't he – a bronze cannon, and he has a green gun carriage. That's why he's liked. Has a star tumbled? No, it's an arrow flying… Ah, how quick, and straight to my heart!… Who was it shooting? You, Sonyechka?"

He bent his head and started whispering incoherent words. I glanced at Yelisei: he was standing with his hands behind his back, gazing pitifully at his gentleman.

"Well then, old fellow, have you become a practical man?" he suddenly asked, directing such a clear, such a conscious look at me, that I gave an involuntary start and was about to reply, but he continued straight away: "Well I, old fellow, haven't become a practical man, I haven't, what can you do? I was born a dreamer, a dreamer! A dream, a dream... What is a dream? Sobakevich's peasant* – that's a dream. Oh!..."

Pasynkov raved almost right through until morning; at last he quietened down little by little, sank back onto his pillow and began to doze. I returned to my own room. Worn out by the cruel night I fell into a deep sleep.

Yelisei woke me up once again.

"Ah, sir!" he began, with a tremor in his voice. "I do believe Yakov Ivanych is dying."

I ran in to Pasynkov. He was lying motionless. By the light of the breaking day he already seemed like a dead man. He recognized me.

"Farewell," he whispered, "give her my greetings, I'm dying..."

"Yasha!" I exclaimed, "enough of that! You're going to live..."

"No, how could I! I'm dying... Here, take this as a memento..." (He pointed at his chest.) "What's that?" he suddenly began. "Just look: the sea... all golden, and upon it blue islands, marble temples, palm trees, incense..."

He fell silent... stretched himself out...

Half an hour later he was no more. Yelisei fell sobbing at his feet. I closed his eyes.

Round his neck he had a small silk amulet on a black lace. I took it for myself.

He was buried on the third day... The noblest heart was hidden for ever in the grave! I myself threw the first handful of earth on top of him.

3

ANOTHER YEAR AND A HALF went by. Business matters compelled me to visit Moscow. I put up in one of the good hotels there. One day, while walking along the corridor, I glanced at the blackboard with the guests' names on it and almost cried out in astonishment: written clearly in chalk against room number twelve stood the name of Sofia Nikolayevna Asanova. I had recently chanced to hear a lot of bad things about her husband; I had learnt that he had developed a passion for wine and cards, was ruined financially and was generally behaving badly. His wife was spoken of with respect… Not without excitement did I return to my room. A passion that had long grown cold seemed to stir in my heart, which began beating hard. I made up my mind to go and see Sofia Nikolayevna. "How much time has passed since the day of our parting!" I thought. "She's probably forgotten everything that happened between us then."

I sent Yelisei, whom I had taken into my service after Pasynkov's death, to leave her my visiting card, and told him to ask whether she was at home and whether I could see her. Yelisei soon returned and announced that Sofia Nikolayevna was at home and receiving visitors.

I set off to see Sofia Nikolayevna. When I went in, she was standing in the middle of the room and saying goodbye to some tall, thickset gentleman. "As you wish," he was saying in a deep, booming voice, "he is not an unharmful man, he is an unproductive man; and in a well-ordered society an unproductive man is harmful, harmful, harmful!"

With these words the tall gentleman left. Sofia Nikolayevna turned to me.

"It's such a long time since we last met!" she said. "Please, do take a seat..."

We sat down. I looked at her... To see after a long separation the features of a face that was once dear, perhaps beloved, and to recognize, yet not recognize them, as if through the former, still not forgotten appearance there protruded another that, albeit similar, is alien; to notice instantly, almost involuntarily, the traces applied by time – this is all rather sad. "And I too must have changed," everyone thinks to himself...

True, Sofia Nikolayevna had not aged a lot; but when I had seen her for the last time she had just turned sixteen, and since then nine years had passed. Her features had become even more regular and severe; as before, they expressed sincerity of feelings and firmness, but instead of the former calm, they spoke of some concealed pain and anxiety. Her eyes had deepened and darkened. She had begun to resemble her mother...

Sofia Nikolayevna was the first to strike up a conversation.

"We've both altered," she began. "Where have you been all this time?"

"Roaming here and there," I replied. "And have you been living in the country all the time?"

"For the most part in the country. Even now I'm only passing through here."

"What of your parents?"

"My mother has passed away, but my father is still in St Petersburg; my brother's in the civil service; Varya lives with them."

"And your spouse?"

"My husband?" she started speaking in a rather hurried voice. "He's in southern Russia now, at the fairs. He always loved horses, you know, and he's set up his own stud... so in order to... he's now buying horses."

At this moment there came into the room a girl of about eight with a Chinese hairstyle, with a very sharp and lively little face and large dark-grey eyes. Upon seeing me, she immediately stretched out her little leg, dropped a nimble curtsy and went up to Sofia Nikolayevna.

"Here, let me present my daughter to you," said Sofia Nikolayevna, touching the little girl under her rounded chin with her finger, "she didn't want to stay at home for anything and persuaded me to bring her with me."

The little girl looked me over with her quick eyes and screwed them up just slightly.

"She's a good girl," continued Sofia Nikolayevna, "she's not afraid of anything. And her studies are going well; I have to praise her for that."

"*Comment se nomme monsieur?*"* asked the little girl in a low voice, leaning towards her mother.

Sofia Nikolayevna gave my name. The little girl glanced at me again.

"What's your name?" I asked her.

"My name's Lydia," the little girl replied, looking me boldly in the eye.

"I expect they spoil you," I remarked.

"Who spoils me?"

"What do you mean, *who*? I expect everybody does, beginning with your parents." (The little girl looked at her mother in silence.) "I imagine Konstantin Alexandrych..." I continued.

"Yes, yes," Sofia Nikolayevna joined in, while her daughter kept her attentive gaze fixed on her. "My husband, of course... he's very fond of children."

A strange expression flashed across Lydia's intelligent little face. Her lips pouted slightly; her head dropped.

"Tell me," added Sofia Nikolayevna, hurriedly, "you're here on business, are you?"

"That's right... And you too?"

"Yes... In your husband's absence, you understand, you get involved in business, like it or not."

"*Maman!*" Lydia tried to begin.

"*Quoi, mon enfant?*"

"*Non – rien... Je te dirai après.*"*

Sofia Nikolayevna laughed and shrugged one shoulder.

We were both silent for a while, and Lydia crossed her arms on her chest with an air of importance.

"Tell me, please," Sofia Nikolayevna began once more, "I seem to remember, you used to have a friend... what was his name now? He had such a kind face... He was always reading poetry; such an enthusiast..."

"Do you mean Pasynkov?"

"Yes, yes, Pasynkov... where is he now?"

"He's dead."

"Dead?" repeated Sofia Nikolayevna. "What a shame!..."

"Did I see him?" asked the little girl, in a hasty whisper.

"No, Lydia, you didn't. What a shame!" Sofia Nikolayevna repeated.

"You feel regret for him..." I began, "so what if you had known him as I knew him?... But may I ask why you started speaking of him in particular?"

"I really don't know..." (Sofia Nikolayevna lowered her eyes.) "Lydia," she added, "go to your nurse."

"Will you call me when the time comes?" asked the little girl.

"Yes, I will."

The little girl left the room. Sofia Nikolayevna turned to me: "Please tell me all you know about Pasynkov."

I began telling her. I outlined in brief the whole of my friend's life, tried, as far as I could, to portray his soul, and described his last meeting with me, his death.

"And that's what sort of a man," I exclaimed, finishing my story, "has left us, unnoticed, scarcely appreciated! And that may not be such a bad thing. What does the appreciation of men signify? But I'm hurt, I'm offended by the fact that such a man, with such a loving and devoted heart, died without once experiencing the bliss of requited love, without exciting sympathy in a single female heart worthy of him!... No matter if men like me don't taste that bliss:

we're unworthy of it; but Pasynkov!... And, what's more, haven't I met in my lifetime a thousand people who couldn't compare with him in any respect, yet who have been loved? Surely one doesn't have to think that certain deficiencies – brashness, for example, or frivolity – are essential in a man for a woman to become attached to him? Or is love afraid of perfection, such perfection as is possible on earth, as something alien and terrible?"

Sofia Nikolayevna heard me out without taking her severe and penetrating eyes off me and keeping her lips tightly pursed; only her brows were occasionally knitted.

"Why do you assume," she said after a short silence, "that not a single woman fell in love with your friend?"

"Because I know it, I know it for certain."

Sofia Nikolayevna wanted to say something, but stopped. She seemed to be struggling with herself.

"You're mistaken," she began at last. "I know a woman who fell ardently in love with your late friend; she loves and remembers him to this day... and word of his death will affect her deeply."

"Who is this woman, may I know?"

"My sister, Varya."

"Varvara Nikolayevna!" I exclaimed in astonishment.

"Yes."

"What? Varvara Nikolayevna?" I repeated. "That..."

"I'll finish your thought out loud," Sofia Nikolayevna continued: "that – in your view – cold, indifferent, limp girl loved your friend: that's why she hasn't got married, nor will. Until today I alone knew about this: Varya would sooner die than reveal her secret. We know how to suffer in silence in our family."

I looked at Sofia Nikolayevna intently for a long time, involuntarily reflecting on the bitter significance of her last words.

"You've surprised me," I said at last. "But do you know, Sofia Nikolayevna, if I were not afraid of arousing unpleasant memories for you, I in my turn could surprise you too..."

"I don't understand you," she said, slowly and with a certain embarrassment.

"You certainly don't understand me," I said, hurrying to get up, "and for that reason, instead of a verbal explanation, allow me to send you something..."

"But what is it?" she asked.

"Don't worry, Sofia Nikolayevna, It's nothing to do with me."

I bowed and returned to my room, got out the amulet that I had taken off Pasynkov, and sent it to Sofia Nikolayevna with the following note:

My late friend wore this amulet constantly on his breast, and he died with it on. Inside it is a note of yours to him, utterly insignificant in content; you can read it. He wore it because he loved you passionately, something he admitted to me only on the eve of his death. Now that he is dead, why should you not learn that his heart too belonged to you?

Yelisei soon returned and brought me back the amulet.

"What?" I asked. "Didn't she ask you to say anything to me?"

"Nothing, sir."

I was silent for a moment.

"Did she read my note?"

"She must have done, sir; her maid took it to her."

"Untouchable!" I thought, remembering Pasynkov's last words.

"Well, off you go," I said out loud.

Yelisei gave a strange sort of smile and did not leave the room.

"A young woman," he began, "has come to see you, sir."

"What young woman?"

Yelisei was silent for a moment.

"Didn't the late master say anything to you, sir?"

"No... What is it?"

"When he was in Novgorod," he continued, putting his hand on the lintel, "he became acquainted with, roughly speaking, a young woman. And now this young woman wants to see you, sir. I met her in the street the other day. I said to her: 'You come along; if the master tells me to, I'll let you in.'"

"Ask her in, ask her in, of course. But then... what sort of woman is she?"

"Ordinary, sir... a townswoman... Russian."

"Did the late Yakov Ivanych love her?"

"He quite loved her, sir. Well, and she... When she heard the master had passed away, she was ever so upset. She's alright, she's a good girl, sir."

"Ask her in, ask her in."

Yelisei left the room, then came back straight away. Behind him walked a young woman in a multicoloured cotton print dress with a dark shawl on her head that covered half her face. When she saw me, she became embarrassed and turned away.

"What's the matter?" Yelisei said to her. "Go on, don't be afraid."

I went up to her and took her by the hand.

"What's your name?" I asked her.

"Masha," she replied in a quiet voice, stealing a glance at me.

To look at, she appeared to be about twenty-two or twenty-three; she had a round, quite ordinary, but pleasant face, delicate cheeks, meek blue eyes and small hands, very pretty and clean. She was neatly dressed.

"You knew Yakov Pasynkov?" I continued.

"I did know him, sir," she said, pulling at the ends of her shawl, and tears welled up in her eyes...

I asked her to take a seat.

She sat down at once on the edge of a chair, without excessive shyness or false modesty. Yelisei left the room.

"You met in Novgorod?"

"Yes, sir, in Novgorod," she replied, folding her hands beneath her shawl. "I only learnt of his death two days ago from Yelisei Timofeyich, sir. When he left for Siberia, Yakov Ivanych promised to write, and he wrote twice, but didn't write any more, sir. I would have followed him even to Siberia, sir, but he didn't want me to."

"Do you have relatives in Novgorod?"

"Yes."

"Have you been living with them?"

"I used to live with my mother and my married sister; but then my mother got angry with me, and my sister began to feel cramped too: they've got a lot of children; so I moved out. I always pinned my hopes on Yakov Ivanych and wanted nothing other than to see him, and he was always kind to me – you can ask Yelisei Timofeyich."

Masha was silent for a moment.

"I've even got his letters," she continued. "Here, sir, look."

She took several letters from her pocket and passed them to me.

"Read them, sir," she added.

I opened up one letter and recognized Pasynkov's handwriting.

> *Dear Masha!* (He wrote in a large, clear hand.) *Yesterday you leant your little head against mine, and when I asked: why are you doing that? you said to me: I want to listen to what you're thinking. I'll tell you what I was thinking: I was thinking how good it would be to teach Masha to read and write! She'd be able to make out this letter...*

Masha glanced at the letter.

"He wrote me that while he was still in Novgorod, sir," she said, "when he was meaning to teach me to read and write. Look at the others, sir. There's one there from Siberia, sir. Read that one, sir."

I read the letters. They were all very affectionate, even tender. In one of them, to be precise, in the first letter from Siberia, Pasynkov called Masha his best friend, promised to send her money for the journey to Siberia and ended with the following words:

I kiss your pretty little hands; the girls here don't have such hands; and their heads are no match for yours, and neither are their hearts... Read the books I gave you and remember me, and I shan't forget you. You alone, only you have loved me: and so I want to belong to you alone too...

"I see he was very attached to you," I said, returning the letters to her.

"He loved me very much," said Masha, putting the letters away carefully in her pocket, and tears began to flow quietly down her cheeks. "I always put my hope in him; if the Lord had prolonged his life, he wouldn't have abandoned me. God grant him eternal life!..."

She wiped her eyes with the end of her shawl.

"And where are you living now?" I asked.

"I'm here now, in Moscow; I came with a lady, but now I'm without a position. I went to see Yakov Ivanych's auntie, but she's very poor herself. Yakov Ivanych often used to talk to me about you, sir," she added, getting up and bowing, "he was always very fond of you and remembered you. And I met Yelisei Timofeyich two days ago and wondered whether you would like to help me, as I'm left without a position now..."

"With great pleasure, Maria... may I ask your patronymic?"

"Petrovna," replied Masha, looking down.

"I'll do everything I can for you, Maria Petrovna," I continued, "I'm only sorry that I'm just passing through and I don't know many good houses."

Masha sighed.

"Any position would do me, sir... I don't know how to cut dresses, but I can do any kind of sewing, sir... well, and I can look after children too."

"I should give her some money," I thought, "but how am I to do it?"

"Listen, Maria Petrovna," I began, not without embarrassment, "do, please, forgive me, but you know from Pasynkov how friendly I was with him... Won't you allow me to offer you... in the first instance a small sum of money?"

Masha looked at me.

"What, sir?" she asked.

"Do you need some money?" I said.

Masha turned quite red and bent her head.

"What do I need money for?" she whispered. "Better find me a position, sir."

"I'll try to find you a position, but I can't give you a definite reply, and you're wrong to feel ashamed, truly... I'm not some sort of stranger to you, after all... Take it from me in memory of our friend..."

I turned away, hastily took several banknotes from my wallet and offered them to her.

Masha stood motionless, her head lowered still further...

"Do take it," I repeated.

She quietly raised her eyes to look at me, gazed sadly into my face, quietly freed her pale hand from under her shawl and reached it out to me.

I laid the banknotes onto her cold fingers. In silence she hid her hand under the shawl once more and lowered her eyes.

"In future as well, Maria Petrovna," I continued, "if you need anything, please turn directly to me. I'll let you know my address."

"I'm humbly grateful, sir," she said, then after a moment's silence added: "Did he tell you about me, sir?"

"I met him on the eve of his death, Maria Petrovna. But then I don't remember... I think he did."

Masha passed her hand over her hair, rested her cheek on it a little, had a think, and then, saying "Goodbye, sir", she left the room.

I sat down by the table and began thinking bitter thoughts. This Masha, her relations with Pasynkov, his letters, Sofia Nikolayevna's sister's secret love for him... "The poor man, the poor man!" I whispered with a heavy sigh. I recalled the whole of Pasynkov's life, his childhood, his youth, Fräulein Friederiche… "There," I thought, "what a lot you were given by fate, what a lot it gave you to enjoy!"

The next day I called on Sofia Nikolayevna again. I was made to wait in the entrance hall and, when I went in, Lydia was already sitting beside her mother. I realized that Sofia Nikolayevna did not wish to renew the conversation of the day before.

We began talking, about what I really cannot remember – about city gossip, business… Lydia frequently had her say and threw me some sly looks. An amusing air of importance would suddenly become apparent on her mobile little face… The clever little girl must have guessed that her mother had sat her down beside her on purpose.

I rose and began to take my farewell. Sofia Nikolayevna saw me to the door.

"I gave you no reply yesterday," she said, stopping on the threshold, "but what reply could I have given? Our life does not depend on us; but we all of us have one anchor, from which, unless you yourself wish it, you will never break away: a sense of duty."

I inclined my head wordlessly to indicate agreement and said goodbye to the young puritan.

All that evening I remained at home, but I did not think about her: I was thinking, thinking constantly about my dear, unforgettable Pasynkov – about that last of the romantics; and emotions, at times sad, at times tender, pierced my breast with sweet pain and resounded in the strings of my still not entirely obsolete heart… May you rest in peace, impractical man, good-natured idealist! And God grant all practical gentlemen, to whom you were always alien and who will now perhaps even laugh at your shadow, God grant they all taste but a hundredth part of those pure pleasures by which, in defiance of fate and men, your poor and humble life was enriched!

Notes

p. 7, *Entbehren sollst du, sollst entbehren*: "Deny yourself, yourself deny" (German), from Goethe's *Faust* (Part I).

p. 11, *a perfect Farnese Hercules*: A third-century Roman sculpture acquired in the sixteenth century by the Farnese family.

p. 12, *Manon Lescaut*: The eponymous heroine of the novel of 1733 by Abbé Prévost (1697–1763).

p. 12, *D'Arlincourt's The Hermit*: *Le Solitaire* by C-V.P. d'Arlincourt (2nd edition, 1821) was in Turgenev's library on his estate at Spasskoye.

p. 12, *en raccourci*: "In brief" (French).

p. 13, *Candide... Paysan perverti etc.*: The works referred to are *Candide*, Voltaire's short novel of 1759; a Russian translation from the German of *The Triumphant Chameleon, or A Portrait of the Anecdotes and Characteristics of Count Mirabeau* appeared in Moscow in 1792; and *The Perverted Peasant* (1776) by Rétif de la Bretonne (1734–1806).

p. 13, *Ce livre... de Lavrine*: "This book belongs to Mademoiselle Yevdokia Lavrina" (French).

p. 13, *Fräulein Clara Stich... absolutely everything*: Clara Stich (1820-62) and Karl Seydelmann (1793–1843) were both held in high regard by Russian theatre-goers in Berlin in the 1830s and 1840s, while Anton Henryk Radziwill (1775–1833) set many of Goethe's pieces to music; his score for *Faust* was first performed in Berlin in 1835.

p. 14, *my friend Horatio*: Hamlet's closest friend and confidant in Shakespeare's play.

p. 17, *about five versts*: A verst was a Russian measure of length approximately equivalent to one kilometre.

p. 17, *a Trasteverino*: An inhabitant of the district of Trastevere in Rome.

p. 24, *George Sand*: French novelist George Sand (1804–76) had the reputation in conservative circles in Russia of an advocate of immoral behaviour in women, but Turgenev was a warm admirer of her work.

p. 26, *I start... feel ashamed*: A slight misquotation from Alexander Pushkin's poem 'A Conversation between Bookseller and Poet' (1824).

p. 36, *A good man... lies*: From 'The Prologue in Heaven', *Faust*, Part I.

p. 37, *Onegin*: Pushkin's novel in verse *Eugene Onegin* (1823–31), depicting the failure of hero and heroine to find love together, was a major influence on much of Turgenev's work.

p. 38, *So cloak me... at rest*: The third stanza the poem 'The day is closing, night draws near' (1851) by Fyodor Tyutchev (1803–73).

p. 40, *Freu't euch des Lebens*: "Rejoice in life" (German).

p. 40, *On the waters... stars*: From the poem entitled '*Auf den See*' ('On the Lake').

p. 42, *Franklin*: Sir John Franklin (1786–1847) perished in his attempt to discover the Northwest Passage between the Atlantic and Pacific Oceans. Many expeditions were organized in subsequent years to search for traces of his ships and their crews.

p. 45, *Manon Lescauts, Fretillons*: The reference to the *History of Mademoiselle Cronel, Known as Fretillon, Written by Herself* (1739) by Pierre-Alexandre Gaillard de Bataille (1708–79) alongside Manon Lescaut suggests an image of women of dubious moral character.

p. 55, *like Mazepa to Kochubei*: Turgenev is here alluding to Pushkin's narrative poem set in the reign of Peter the Great, *Poltava* (1828).

p. 56, *What ever does he want... there*: From the final scene of *Faust*, Part I.

p. 62, *Mon cher ami Constantin*: "My dear friend Konstantin" (French).

p. 71, *Yermak's son*: Yermak was a Cossack who participated prominently in Russian expansion into Siberia until his death by drowning in 1585.

p. 72, *Resignation*: Friedrich von Schiller's poem 'Resignation' was a key work for many of Turgenev's Russian contemporaries; the title was variously translated into Russian as, for example, 'Renunciation' or 'Obedience to Fate'.

p. 73, *before "the shrine of beauty"*: "Before the shrine of beauty" is the closing line of Pushkin's poem 'The Beauty' (1832).

p. 73, *Matthison, Uhland*: Friedrich Matthison (1761–1831) and Johann Uhland (1787–1862) were both German poets.

p. 73, *mein lieber, lieber Herr Jacob*: "My dear, dear Mr Yakov" (German).

p. 75, *Above us... their Maker*: This is a slight misquotation from the poem 'To My Friend V.A. Zh[ukovsky]' (1825) by Ivan Kozlov (1779–1840).

p. 78, *The Stars*: 'The Stars' is Franz Schubert's 1811 setting of a poem by Friedrich Klopstock (1724–1803).

p. 90, *Aesculapius*: In Greek mythology, Aesculapius, a son of Apollo, the god of medicine, was himself a healer and physician who became a demigod.

p. 91, *Now once more... to kiss*: The first lines are the opening to Pushkin's poem 'Presentiment' (1828), and the second quotation is the opening to his poem 'Leave-taking' (1830).

p. 91, *There is a girl who lives nearby*: A line from the poem 'The Testament' (1841) by Mikhail Lermontov (1814–41).

p. 92, *I have not much time... upon this earth*: Another line from 'The Testament' (see note above).

p. 93, *The whole of our life... dreaming*: The allusion is to *Life is a Dream* (1635) by Pedro Calderón de la Barca, a play much admired by Turgenev.

p. 95, *Sobakevich's peasant*: Sobakevich is a character in Nikolai Gogol's epic *Dead Souls* (1842) whose imagination endows dead peasants with exaggerated qualities.

p. 98, *Comment se nomme monsieur*: "What's the gentleman's name?" (French).

p. 99, *Maman... dirai après*: "Mummy!"; "What, my child?"; "No, it's nothing... I'll tell you later." (French)

Extra Material

on

Ivan Turgenev's

Faust

Ivan Turgenev's Life

Birth and Background

Ivan Sergeyevich Turgenev was born in the Russian city of Oryol on 9th November 1818 (all dates in this section follow the Gregorian calendar). His mother, the wealthy Varvara Petrovna Lutovinova, according to many reports was an extremely capricious and cruel woman. Her baronial estate of Spasskoye contained twenty villages, and she had control of five thousand serfs; she is reported to have had some of her serfs deported to Siberia because they did not take their hats off in her presence, and to have regularly inflicted corporal punishments on them. She came into her inheritance at the age of twenty-six, and three years later married a twenty-three-year-old army officer, Sergei Turgenev, from an ancient family of aristocrats who had fallen on hard times: he possessed only one village and had just a hundred and thirty serfs. He married her presumably for her money: he seems to have taken very little interest in her afterwards, spending his time in numerous affairs with women, mainly serf girls at Spasskoye and his own estate, Turgenevo.

Ivan Turgenev had an older brother, Nikolai, who was born in 1816, and a younger brother, Sergei, who was born in 1821; very little is known about this last child, but it appears he was partially paralysed, epileptic and mentally retarded; he died in his teens.

Childhood

Varvara Petrovna's already unpleasant personality became, it seems, progressively worse as a result of her husband's philandering, and Ivan recounted later that he and Nikolai had been whipped and beaten almost daily during their childhoods, frequently as a result of a whim on their mother's part.

As in most Russian upper-class families of the time, French was spoken as the language of preference; indeed, Russian was considered among this class to be a barbaric language.

Therefore Turgenev was from an early age fluent in French, and also acquired a good knowledge of German from private tutors. Fortunately for his career as a writer in Russian, his parents almost totally ignored their sons, leaving Ivan ample time to roam around the locality getting to know the peasants and play with their children. It was from them that Turgenev learnt spoken Russian: he later claimed that he was taught to read and write Russian by his father's valet.

Move to Moscow

By 1827 the whole family had moved to Moscow, where the boys were enrolled at a private academy. However, after a couple of years, Nikolai was transferred to the Military Officer Training School in Petersburg, and Ivan was brought back home to have his education completed by tutors who would prepare him for the university entrance exams. By the age of eleven, Turgenev was being given lessons in French, German, Maths and Philosophy, and already trying his hand at writing poetry and dramas in the "sublime" style of pre-Pushkin Russian authors.

University and Ill Health

Turgenev entered Moscow University in 1833, but lasted there only one term. Just before entering university, he had been bedridden for some months by an unknown illness, probably of a hypochondriac nature, and having missed too much time from his initial term he was transferred in autumn 1835 to the Philological Faculty of Petersburg University. On 11th September of that year, when Turgenev was only sixteen, his father died.

Although intending to become a university academic, probably in Philosophy, he was already writing Romantic poetic dramas in the manner of Byron. When he sent one of them to a leading literary magazine, it was rejected, but with some encouraging words from the editor, and in 1838 he did have two poems published in this periodical. As part of his studies, he had now begun to learn English, and he attempted to translate extracts from *King Lear*, *Othello* and Byron's *Manfred*. Besides English, Turgenev was devoting a great deal of his time to studying Latin and Ancient Greek. He also took private lessons in painting and drawing, and became an accomplished artist and caricaturist.

Stay in Berlin

Turgenev graduated from the Faculty of History and Philology in June 1837. His mother thought that the true fount of all learning was outside Russia, so in May 1838 she sent him to do extra study in the subject at the University of

Berlin. On the crossing from Stettin to Berlin the ferry caught fire, and Turgenev offered some of the sailors large bribes to let him embark on a lifeboat before anybody else, including women and children – an incident that was to haunt and embarrass him for the rest of his life.

In Berlin he devoted himself intensively to the study of Philosophy, History, Latin and Greek. He fell under the spell of Hegel's philosophy, and soon became involved in the seething discussion groups regularly held by the students. There were a large number of young Russians studying in Germany: the vast majority of these were social progressives who wanted a total transformation of the social and political situation at home – often by violent revolutionary means, including assassination. Among the people he met in Berlin was Mikhail Bakunin, one of the founders of the Russian anarchist movement. Although Turgenev held intense philosophical discussions with him, and was at first attracted by Bakunin's charismatic personality, he managed to keep his distance intellectually and maintain a moderate stance in regard to the methods of achieving social change. Some contemporary critics claimed that the figure of Rudin, the eponymous hero of Turgenev's first novel, was a portrait – in fact, a caricature – of Mikhail Bakunin.

Return to Russia

In the spring of 1841 Turgenev returned to Russia. In the meantime, his mother's mansion at Spasskoye had been burnt down by a fire, apparently caused by a peasant woman performing a propitiatory ritual with hot coals. Only one wing was left, and Turgenev had to be content with one room there until the end of the summer. In the winter of that year, his elder brother Nikolai married one of his mother's parlour maids. Varvara Petrovna immediately stopped his allowance, and Nikolai was forced to resign his officer's commission in the army and get a lowly job in the civil service. She severed all contact with him for many years. Ivan enrolled again at Petersburg University and began to study for a Master's in Philosophy which would have enabled him to gain a university post. He moved into his brother's flat and, after a period of intense studies, passed the exams successfully in June 1842. He then travelled to Moscow to apply for the vacant Chair of Philosophy at Moscow University.

Love Life

However, he never submitted this application, as Turgenev's personal life underwent a dramatic change. In May 1842 he had had a brief affair with a sempstress employed by his mother. She became pregnant by him, and his mother threw them out of the house. He found a room for her in Moscow, and settled an allowance on her. She soon bore him a daughter who was given the humble peasant name of Pelageya. At the same time, Turgenev met in Moscow Bakunin's sister Tatyana, who was even more imbued with Hegelian ideals than her brother. She claimed that, though she loved Turgenev, she simply wanted to be his "sister" and his "friend". This Platonic relationship lasted for two years, by which time it seems Turgenev had become thoroughly disillusioned with Tatyana, Bakunin, Hegelianism and philosophy in general.

Parasha and the Birth of a Literary Career

Turgenev gave up any ambition of becoming an academic, and took a civil-service job at the Ministry of Interior. But he also began now to devote more time to writing, and one of his first mature works was a long narrative poem entitled *Parasha*. The poem, written in clear and simple language, in imitation of Pushkin, tells the tale of a love affair among ordinary peasant folk. The Romantic subjects and flowery style of his younger years had been left behind – as it turned out, for ever. *Parasha* was published in 1843 at the author's own expense, and the renowned critic Belinsky described it as one of the most remarkable productions of the year. Following this, Turgenev and Belinsky became close friends, and the critic introduced the author into the literary circles of Petersburg and Moscow.

Reprimanded by his office superiors for being often late for work or not turning up at all, Turgenev decided to resign his job and devote himself entirely to literature. His mother, in disgust, cut off his allowance and all contact with him for several years. During this period, Turgenev had to live on practically nothing, in unheated rooms, even during the Russian winter.

Pauline Viardot

In 1843 occurred an event that was to prove the decisive turning point of Turgenev's life, and that caused him to spend much of the rest of his life outside Russia. The world-renowned Spanish opera singer Pauline Viardot, née García, visited Petersburg to sing at its opera houses. She was married to Louis Viardot, a man twenty years older than herself. Turgenev met her for the first time in November 1843, and became immediately infatuated with her. This passion was to remain with him for the rest of his life, making it difficult for him to form a stable relationship with any other woman. During Pauline's first visit to Russia, Turgenev had only a brief contact with her, as she was constantly monopolized by her many other long-standing admirers. Turgenev was able to see Pauline again when she came back to sing in Petersburg the following year, but he was once more almost ignored by her, though he inveigled himself into a long and animated conversation with her husband.

Travels Abroad

In February 1845 Turgenev went abroad, allegedly to consult an eminent oculist, but in fact to follow the Viardots to Paris, having received an invitation from Pauline to spend a short time at her country chateau of Courtavenel. He was by now writing affectionate letters to her; her letters to him were far more intermittent and reserved.

Turgenev spent much of the next few years abroad. While in France in 1845, he began to write, from his own experiences, stories of Russian peasant life, portraying the cruelty suffered by serfs from their landowners. These sketches, for the most part originally printed in Russian literary journals, were finally collected and published in volume form in August 1852 as *Memoirs of a Hunter.*

Turgenev once again saw Pauline singing in Petersburg in 1846, and then left Russia with the Viardots in early 1847. From then on, for the rest of his life, he would spend long periods of time with Pauline and her husband in France, Germany and Britain, always remaining on friendly terms with her husband. There is little evidence as to whether Pauline and Ivan ever consummated their relationship. Paul, the child born to Pauline in 1857, may well have been Turgenev's son, although she frequently had other lovers.

Turgenev was in Paris for the latter part of the 1848 revolution. The first upheaval had seen the monarchy being overthrown and replaced by a bourgeois government. Afterwards there had been further turmoil on the streets when the workers, in their turn, tried to obtain concessions from the new administration. Turgenev, while declaring at first his full sympathy with those who brought down the monarchy and then with those who tried to establish a more democratic government, was sickened by the needless violence of the intellectual revolutionaries who incited the working classes to man the barricades, leading to many of them being slaughtered by government troops.

Return to Russia

In the summer of 1850, Turgenev finally left Paris and went back to Russia. In the preceding years he had written most of the sketches for *Memoirs of a Hunter* as well as several plays, which are generally considered to be among his weaker works, with the exception of *A Month in the Country*. The play, heavily cut by the censor, was published in a drastically altered version in January 1855 and premiered in its fuller, uncensored version in Moscow only in 1872.

While Turgenev was in France, his mother had repeatedly appealed to him to return home, and when he refused, she had devised a vicious way of punishing him, forcing his daughter Pelageya, now seven years old, to work in the kitchen with the other servants. When he returned home and discovered the situation, Turgenev immediately withdrew Pelageya from Spasskoye, and wrote to Pauline Viardot asking whether the singer could accept his daughter into her family. Pauline accepted, and Pelageya was dispatched to France, promptly renamed Paulinette, provided with tutors and brought up as a French lady.

Mother's Death and Inheritance

Varvara Petrovna became suddenly ill and died on 10th December 1850. The estates and wealth were divided between Ivan and his elder brother Nikolai, leaving the writer with the whole of Spasskoye. Proving the sincerity of his democratic ideals, he emancipated all his serfs and gave them reasonable financial severance payments – a move that was considered revolutionary at the time. If they wished to remain on his land they could pay him a moderate rent and farm it for their own profit, rather than having to turn over most of their produce to him.

Imprisonment and Exile

In March 1852 the famous writer Gogol had died, and Turgenev published a brief obituary in the press. Although by the end of his life Gogol had become profoundly reactionary and Turgenev's article contained nothing of a political nature, but simply spoke glowingly of his works, the Tsarist government reacted angrily and sentenced Turgenev to a month in prison. At the end of that term, he was sent back to Spasskoye for a two-year period of house arrest. Turgenev spent this time writing, reading and hunting on his estate. In April 1853, he wrote to the Crown Prince Alexander acknowledging his guilt and asking for permission to leave the estate in order to consult doctors. The permission was finally granted by the Tsar in November that year, meaning that Turgenev had only served sixteen months of his sentence. However, he was kept under police surveillance until 1856.

In August 1852 *Memoirs of a Hunter* had appeared in volume form, and it was an instant success. One alarmed aristocrat described it as "an incendiary work", and the Tsar, Nicholas I, dismissed the censor who had authorized its publication.

First Novel

Turgenev now began to experiment with longer forms, such as novellas and novels. On 17th June 1855, he sat down to write his first novel, *Rudin*, and completed it in only seven weeks. It was published, with considerable additions, in the January and February 1856 issues of the literary journal *Sovremennik* (*The Contemporary*).

Illness and Despair

In 1856 Turgenev spent the summer at Spasskoye, then travelled to France to be with the Viardots. His time there was embittered by the realization that Pauline was having an affair with the artist Ary Scheffer. Possibly as a result of Viardot's unfaithfulness, Turgenev was often ill with what appears to be some kind of psychosomatic illness, of which a major symptom was agonizing pains in his bladder. He suffered from this illness for many years afterwards, and there is speculation he may have become impotent as a result of it. He and Pauline had a big argument towards the end of 1856, and his affliction became even worse, plaguing him for another sixteen months or so. Turgenev lost his interest in writing and was plunged into despair, possibly suffering a mild nervous breakdown. He spent most of this period lodging in Paris, with occasional visits to Germany, Britain and Italy. On a visit to London in May 1857, he had repeated contact with such luminaries as Disraeli, Thackeray, Macaulay and Carlyle: by this time his English was competent enough for him to engage in long conversations on literature and politics with those he met there.

In October 1856 Turgenev began to write *Home of the Gentry*. Owing to his mental and physical sufferings, work proceeded very slowly, and the novel was completed only in the autumn of 1858. It was published in January 1859 in *Sovremennik* and was an immediate success. On a brief return to Russia, Turgenev found himself lionized in literary society.

In June 1858, Viardot's lover, Ary Scheffer, died suddenly. Although Turgenev wrote to her a couple of times soon afterwards expressing his condolences, he did not send her any more letters until April 1859, just before he returned to France, perhaps because relationships between them had greatly deteriorated. Even when he did return, he saw little of Viardot, and she kept him at a distance.

On the Eve

During this period, Turgenev was able to begin a new novel, *On the Eve*, which was almost finished by the time he went back to Russia in October 1859. It was published in the January and February 1860 editions of the periodical *Russkiy Vestnik* (*Russian Herald*). Generally approved by the critics for its style, the novel was criticized by some for the absence of any social viewpoint and for not attempting to stimulate readers to improve the social conditions surrounding them.

Fathers and Children and the Critical Backlash

Between May 1860 and May 1861, Turgenev spent most of his time in France, except for a brief visit to Britain and a few weeks on the Isle of Wight in August 1860. It was here that, as he swam off the beach at Ventnor, the first idea for his next novel, *Fathers and Children*, occurred to him. He swiftly set about drawing up the characters, and then working out a detailed story around this germ of an idea. The first draft of the novel was completed at Spasskoye on 11th August 1861; then, in September that year, on his return to Paris he began revising it extensively. Published in Russia in February 1862, *Fathers and Children* unleashed a torrent of abuse from all sides that Turgenev simply had not anticipated. The right-wing press vilified him for daring to take the radical and free-thinking younger generation as its heroes, while the radicals saw the representatives of this generation in the novel, particularly the young doctor Bazarov, as caricatures of themselves. Incidentally, Bazarov describes himself as a "nihilist", a word which, although not unknown in Russian before, was popularized by Turgenev with this novel: following its publication, many of the younger generation ostentatiously adopted this label for themselves. In Turgenev's usage, it implies not so much somebody who believes in nothing, but a person who takes none of the commonly accepted beliefs on trust, subjecting everything to analysis by intensive reasoning. Years later, Turgenev wrote to a correspondent that he regretted giving what he called the "reactionary rabble" this word to beat the younger generation with.

Move to Baden-Baden

Viardot and her husband had in the meantime moved to a villa near the fashionable German spa town of Baden-Baden, so in 1863 Turgenev settled in this town too, living there until 1871, with the exception of a few brief visits back to Russia. In the spring of 1862, Viardot had resumed contact with him, possibly because she wanted him to help her select a number of Russian poems she could set to music and use his influence to sell them for her in Russia.

Problems with Russian Authorities

At this time, Turgenev was still under suspicion from the Russian authorities. On a visit to England in May 1862, he had met up with a number of Russian radicals based in London, and discussed their ideas with them. This became known in Russia, and he was summoned back there to be tried for his association with these people or face the risk of having all his property confiscated. He wrote a letter to the Tsar in person, in which he said that he had never expressed his political opinions by violent means, but had explained them in all moderation in his works. Back in Russia, in September 1863 he appeared before a court consisting of members of the Senate, and all charges were immediately dropped. Herzen and Bakunin, however, two of the revolutionaries based in London, in their publications accused Turgenev of having compromised himself by writing to the Tsar, and have betrayed his old ideals. To make up for the contempt with which he was regarded by some of his Russian contemporaries, Turgenev became acquainted with famous French authors such as Gustave Flaubert, whom he first met in January 1863.

Smoke

In 1862, Turgenev had started drafting detailed plans and character sketches for another novel, *Smoke*. He began writing it in November 1865, and finished it in January 1866. After lengthy discussions with the editorial board of the *Russian Herald* as to the work's political and moral content, the book was published in March 1867. *Smoke* takes place largely outside Russia, and one of its major characters, a Russian called Potugin, who is vaguely reminiscent of Turgenev, is a passionate Westernizer contemptuous of the Russian mentality. Not surprisingly, this provoked a storm in Russia, where the press accused Turgenev of a total lack of patriotism.

Move to England

The Franco-Prussian War of 1870–71, and the resulting growth of aggressive anti-French feelings in Germany, meant that Pauline Viardot, whose husband was French, no longer felt safe living there. The family moved to England in the autumn of 1870, and settled there till the end of the war. Turgenev, although as a Russian he had no reason to feel unsafe in Germany, faithfully followed them to London in November 1870, where he stayed for almost a year. He spent what Henry James – whom he met in Paris four years later – called a "lugubrious" winter in London.

While in England Turgenev was introduced into the leading artistic circles. There he met, among other literary figures, Tennyson, Dante Gabriel Rossetti and Ford Madox Brown, and struck up a close friendship with George Eliot. Although there is no record that he ever spoke to Dickens, it is likely that he met him, since he attended three of his public readings and was enthralled by them. Turgenev's English was by now excellent, and he was invited to Edinburgh to give an address in English at the Walter Scott centenary celebrations in August 1871. While there he went grouse-shooting on the Scottish moors, where he met the poet Robert Browning.

Move to Paris

Turgenev followed the Viardots on their return to Paris in October 1871 and, apart from a few brief spells in Russia, he spent four years living as a guest in the various houses occupied by Pauline and her husband. In 1875, he and the Viardots purchased a large country estate at Bougival, near Saint-Germain-en-Laye, a forty-five-minute ride from Paris. He built himself a Swiss-style chalet on the estate, very close to the manor house where Pauline lived, and it was here at Bougival that he spent the last years of his life. Turgenev now established a very close friendship with Flaubert, and also had frequent contact with George Sand, Zola, Daudet and, some time later, Maupassant.

Virgin Soil a Prophetic Novel

Turgenev spent his time not only writing original prose, but also translating into Russian from French, German and English: for instance, his was the first version into Russian of Flaubert's *Trois Contes*. His last novel, *Virgin Soil*, a book that he had been planning, writing and revising for six years, was published in the January and February 1877 issues of the *European Herald*. He told the editor of this periodical that, in this last novel, he intended to put everything that he thought and felt about the situation in Russia, both about the reactionary and revolutionary camps. The novel was fiercely attacked in the Russian press, with many commentators claiming that the author had now been so long out of his country he had no longer any knowledge of Russian life. However, just a month after the novel's publication, fifty-two young people were arrested for just such activities as Turgenev had described in his book and, exactly as he had foretold, they were put on trial. This created great sympathy for the prisoners both at home and abroad, and *Virgin Soil* became a best-seller in Britain, France and America, with one French critic claiming that Turgenev had shown himself to be a true prophet.

Triumphal Return to Russia

If Turgenev, as a result of the Russian press reaction to his novel, now believed he was despised by the public, including the liberal younger generation, he was mistaken. In January 1879 his brother Nikolai died, and Ivan set off to Russia to oversee the disposal of Nikolai's estate. At a literary gathering, a toast was proposed to him as "the loving instructor of our young people". Turgenev was so staggered at this unexpected reception that he burst into tears. He was invited to meeting after meeting, where he was constantly greeted by thunderous applause, although the authorities still disapproved of him. In Petersburg his hotel was stormed by thousands of people wanting his autograph, or even just a sight of him. He returned to Paris, looking – as friends said – younger and more cheerful. He was now showered with academic honours, including an Honorary Doctorate at Oxford University, for which he travelled to England. The orator at this ceremony declared that his works had led to the emancipation of the Russian serfs.

Illness and Death

Turgenev was by now beginning to feel very unwell. He paid a final brief visit to Russia in February 1880, and spent one further short period in England in October 1881, where he went partridge-shooting at Newmarket, meeting Anthony Trollope, R.D. Blackmore and other writers.

On 3rd May the following year, he wrote to a friend from Bougival that he had been suffering from some kind of angina connected with gout. His shoulders and back ached, and he often had to lie down for long periods. In January 1883 he was operated in Paris for a small tumour in his abdomen. But his condition continued to worsen: he was in intolerable pain and had become very emaciated. His illness was at last diagnosed as incurable cancer of the spine. By now he was bedridden at Bougival, and on 1st September 1883 he slipped into unconsciousness, dying two days later. His body, unaccompanied by Pauline Viardot, was transported to Petersburg. The funeral service was held in the Cathedral of Our Lady of Kazan, and a vast funeral procession followed the coffin to the Volkovo Cemetery in Petersburg, where Turgenev was buried on 9th October.

Ivan Turgenev's Works

Juvenilia

As mentioned before, Turgenev's early works were mainly poems in the high-flown classical style of pre-Pushkin Russian writers. However, he swiftly turned against these models, and strove to achieve for his mature writings a limpid idiom, including dialogue based on the everyday language of the Russian peasant. In sharp distinction to many of the writers of the time, who explicitly tried to put forward a progressive social message in their works, Turgenev aimed to achieve total objectivity and impersonality. Whilst depicting the sufferings of the working people around him, he limited himself to describing their lives without passing judgement and leaving the readers to draw their own conclusions.

Plays

Turgenev wrote nine plays in all, but the only one to have found a permanent place in the repertoire is *A Month in the Country* (1855). Indeed, after 1857 he virtually abandoned the genre.

A Month in the Country

Turgenev wrote the first version of *A Month in the Country* in 1850. It was originally called *The Student*, then *Two Women*. He sent the manuscript to *Sovremennik*, who agreed to publish it, but the censors demanded drastic cuts, as the speeches of the student Belyayev were too inflammatory, and the motif of a married woman in love with another man was morally impermissible. The censors ordered that she be changed into a widow, and Turgenev reluctantly made the relevant cuts. The play was still turned down, and had to be revised even further. This version was published only in 1855, and does not appear to have ever been staged. It was only with the easing of the political climate under Tsar Alexander II that Turgenev's play was published again in 1869, in a version much closer to his original idea. In the revised text, the widow is once again shown as a wife in love with another man. However, even when it was finally staged in Moscow in 1872, under the title *A Month in the Country*, further revisions had to be made because a few of the speeches were still regarded as too incendiary. The play was not a great success, but in 1879 the renowned young actress Marya Savina chose it for a benefit performance in Petersburg, and asked for just a few short cuts to be made on grounds of length. This time it was a triumph, and immediately entered the repertoire.

A Month in the Country predates Chekhov in its depth of characterization and its skilful depiction of the series of barely perceptible changes that take place over a month in the relationships between the characters, leading, by the end, to their lives being totally altered. The play contrasts two social groups, the old and the young, in what was to become a recurring theme in Turgenev's work: the older gentry living fruitless and frustrated lives, with the younger generation full of hope and idealism – and neither of them attaining happiness.

In the play, Natalya is married to the staid and much older Arkady Islayev, while a "friend of the family", Rakitin, also lives in their country house. Natalya and Arkady are clearly based on

Pauline Viardot and her husband, and Turgenev explicitly stated in a letter that Rakitin represented how Turgenev felt about his own situation with regard to them. Natalya falls in love with a young, idealistic, socially progressive student, Belyayev, whom she has engaged as tutor to her son. Vera, her seventeen-year-old ward, instantly falls in love with him too, but Natalya, as a result of her own feelings for him, forces her into marrying the much older and boring Bolshintsov. Belyayev cannot cope with the intensity of the two women's passions and flees. Rakitin, badly hurt by Natalya's lack of feeling for him, withdraws from the scene, leaving her alone with her husband, whom she respects, but does not love. They return to their aimless, idle lives after this month of emotional turmoil.

Memoirs of a Hunter

The title which first established Turgenev's reputation in Russia was *Memoirs of a Hunter* (which has also been translated as *Sketches of a Huntsman* and *Notes of a Sportsman*). This collection of tales of Russian rural life was mostly written in France and Germany, where Turgenev lived at the end of the 1840s and beginning of the 1850s. It consists of twenty-four stories of between 3,000 and 12,000 words in length, most of them originally published as they were written in *Sovremennik* between 1847 and 1851. Twenty-one sketches were published in volume form in 1852; a further story was added in 1872, and another two in 1874. The tales were drawn from Turgenev's own observations of the appalling living conditions of the peasants and the cruelty imposed by the upper classes on their serfs, which he had witnessed when he had roamed round the countryside in his childhood and when, as a youth, he had gone hunting in the locality. The style of the stories, set against lyrical descriptions of nature, is totally impersonal. The reactionary Tsar Nicholas I dismissed the censor who had permitted the volume's publication, but when he died in 1855, the new Tsar, the reforming Alexander II, is said to have read the book and resolved to free the serfs – which finally happened in 1861. The book was a great success and was immediately reprinted.

The Diary of a Superfluous Man

The Diary of a Superfluous Man (1850) may be considered Turgenev's first novella. It was with this work that he introduced into the Russian consciousness the concept of the "superfluous man", which had played such a large part in Russian literature before and was to appear in many subsequent literary incarnations. The term denotes either a person who has the education and abilities to work for society and improve social and political conditions, but who through lack of willpower never manages to achieve anything, or someone who strives to achieve change but is totally ignored by society and so gives up in baffled disillusionment. The story is a personal account written by a young, well-educated man who has learnt from his doctor that he may be dying of an unnamed illness. He has drifted through life without any goal, has never managed to make much use of his education, or fulfil any of his ambitions, or set up any permanent relationship with the opposite sex. Now, as he may be approaching an early death, he is left to reflect on his wasted life.

Mumu

'Mumu' (1854) was based on an incident which had happened at Spasskoye, and the female landowner of the story represents Turgenev's own mother. A hard-working young peasant, being deaf and dumb, has never managed to marry, and the only thing he can find to love is a young puppy that has been abandoned. As he is unable to speak, Mumu is the only name he can give to it. But the landowner complains that the puppy's barking is keeping her awake at night, and the order goes out, via the steward, to kill it. The peasant takes the dog to a river and, uncomplainingly, drowns the only thing ever to have loved him. However, the story ends with him striding away from his owner's control, and readers are left to draw their own conclusions about what his feelings are at this piece of wanton viciousness on her part.

Faust

Faust (1856) consists of nine letters from a character called Pavel to his friend Semyon. Pavel recounts how, a few years after his first meeting with her, he sees again Vera, now a married woman. She had been brought up in a very strict manner, and forbidden by her mother to read any creative literature, especially poetry. Pavel, now he has met her again, visits her frequently at home, and tries to interest her in literature by reading her Goethe's *Faust*. Her feelings are so inflamed by this first exposure to poetry that she falls in love with Pavel and arranges a tryst with him; however, on the way to her rendezvous, she sees an apparition of her dead mother – possibly caused by her subconscious guilt – falls seriously ill and dies.

Asya

Asya (1858) is a novella set in a small village on the Rhine and, unusually for Turgenev, it contains no implicit social message. The unnamed narrator, a middle-aged Russian, recalls events of twenty years before, when he was on holiday in Germany and met a Russian painter called Gagin, who introduces him to Asya, a girl he claims is his sister. The narrator suspects she is his mistress, but later Gagin tells him she is his illegitimate half-sister, whom he has been bringing up since the death of her parents. Although loving Gagin with the feelings of a sister, she falls passionately in love with the narrator, who baulks at the idea of marrying her and decides to give the matter some prolonged thought. By the time he decides in favour of the relationship, Gagin and Asya have returned to Russia, and he accepts that he has missed his chance of happiness. She writes to him reproachfully, telling him that one word of encouragement from him would have been enough to persuade her to marry him. However, his feelings prove shallow: he doesn't suffer long, and he never hears of her again.

First Love

First Love (1860) is perhaps the most autobiographical of all Turgenev's works. The author claimed that an identical incident had happened to him in his adolescence at Spasskoye. The hero is a boy who falls in love with the slightly older daughter of a young neighbour. Realizing she does not return his feelings and has a lover, the boy takes a knife to attack his rival. However, on drawing near the girl and her lover, he sees to his dismay that it is his own father. He drops the knife and flees mortified, with bitterness having entered his young soul.

King Lear of the Steppe

In *King Lear of the Steppe* (1870), the narrator is an adult who recalls the time he was an adolescent still living on his mother's estates. The tale's main character is one of her serfs, Kharlov, the "King Lear" of the story. He is a man of gigantic stature and strength, a hard-working peasant farmer who lives in a small house he has built with his own hands. The narrator's mother, Kharlov's owner, had married him off at the age of forty to a seventeen-year-old girl who bore him two daughters but then died. The two girls, out of compassion, were subsequently brought up in the narrator's home, but they became cruel and grasping. One night Kharlov has a dream he interprets as a premonition of his coming death, and immediately draws up a will dividing his estate between his two daughters. Just a few weeks later he is evicted by them, and is given refuge by the narrator's mother. But, driven mad, he climbs up onto the roof of the house he had built, which has now passed into other hands, and begins to tear chunks from it. He falls from the roof to his death.

Spring Waters

Based on a chance encounter Turgenev had had with a beautiful young girl in Frankfurt in 1841, *Spring Waters* was published in 1872. As he returns home from a party, the fifty-year-old

Dmitry Sanin reflects on the futility of life. He recalls a time in the 1840s, when he once stopped off in Frankfurt. A beautiful young girl, Gemma, rushes from a building and asks him to help her brother Emilio, who she thinks is dying but has only fainted. When Sanin revives him, he is welcomed into Gemma's household as Emilio's saviour. Sanin cancels his plans to return to Russia, because he is now in love with Gemma, who is unfortunately engaged to be married to a vile old German shopkeeper. But Gemma returns Sanin's love, breaks off her engagement, and she and Sanin agree to marry. He is about to go back to Russia to sell his lands when he meets an old acquaintance, Polozov, who is married to a wealthy and attractive woman. He convinces Sanin that his wife will buy his lands, but she, simply out of malevolence, seduces him in order to wreck his projected marriage. He becomes totally infatuated with her, and writes Gemma a letter breaking off their liaison. Polozov's wife, having achieved her aim, starts to treat him with cold contempt and then discards him, leaving him desolate and with nothing.

Novels

As well as novellas and short stories, Turgenev wrote six novels. The first four were published in the space of just six years, between 1856 and 1862. Possibly as a consequence of the criticism he had received for these works in the Russian press – especially for the fourth, *Fathers and Children* – his following novel appeared only five years later, and the last one ten years after that.

Rudin

Originally entitled *A Highly Gifted Nature*, Turgenev's first novel, *Rudin* (1856), tells the tale of another "superfluous man". He is a well-educated but impecunious young nobleman, who has been educated at Moscow University, as well as in Heidelberg and Berlin. The setting is the country estate of a wealthy noblewoman, Darya Lasunskaya, in a provincial backwater. The charismatic Rudin, whom nobody knows, is introduced into their circle and totally disrupts the settled life of the household, especially affecting the peace of mind of young Natalya. When he leaves, things return to their normal state, but some of the characters have subtly changed for ever. The unexpected entry of an outsider into a social circle and the turmoil it causes is a leitmotif in Turgenev's writings: other examples are Lavretsky in *Home of the Gentry*, Insarov in *On the Eve*, Bazarov in *Fathers and Children* and Belyayev in *A Month in the Country*. The feckless Rudin now moves into Darya's mansion, sponging off the family, and obviously striking up a liaison with her impressionable young daughter Natalya. This budding romance becomes known to Darya, who strongly disapproves of it. Instead of standing up firmly for their love, however, Rudin declares one must "submit to destiny", leaving Natalya hurt, confused and feeling deceived by him. When Rudin departs from the estate, he sends her a letter confessing that he has always been guilty of such indecision.

The final section of the novel portrays events some two years later. Natalya is now engaged to a staid, worthy local landowner, and Rudin is still drifting around Russia, living at the expense of anybody he can latch on to. There is a very short epilogue which is not entirely convincing, and seems to have been appended as an afterthought: Rudin takes the part of the workers manning the barricades in the Paris Insurrection of 1848, which Turgenev had been witness to. He is shot dead by the soldiers, and even in death his sacrifice appears to have been meaningless, as somebody shouts out: "They've got the Pole!" Perhaps the message of this apparently incongruous ending is that, ironically, the first time this aimless Russian nobleman tries to exert himself to do something useful, he dies, and nobody even realizes that he is Russian, or has any personality of his own. He is still just another "superfluous man".

Although the critics noted the novel's lucid prose style, the press reaction was puzzled; the right-wing journals accused Turgenev of disrespecting the upper classes in his portrayal of them as ineffective drifters and spongers, while the radicals thought that Rudin was a satirical portrait of one of them – well-educated, full of fine words, but ineffectual, and able to make no lasting impact on anything. As mentioned before, it was even claimed that Rudin was a caricature of the revolutionary Bakunin, who became one of the founders of the Russian anarchist movement, and whom Turgenev had met when they were both students in Berlin.

Home of the Gentry

Home of the Gentry is Turgenev's second novel. Turgenev had heard, when he was in Rome in 1857, that the Tsarist government was at last considering the question of the emancipation of the serfs, and decided that he should devote himself entirely to depicting the reality of the social situation in Russia in his writings. Accordingly, he started planning *Home of the Gentry*, which was completed in 1858 and published in early 1859. Whereas in *Rudin* he had been portraying an aimless member of the educated upper classes, in his next novel he depicted what he most valued in Russian life and tradition and, unusually for him, looked quite critically at some aspects of Western culture.

The setting is the country house of a wealthy family in the town of O—— (most probably Oryol, the county town of the region where Turgenev was born). This house, and the family's estate, represent here for Turgenev an oasis of peace and stability amidst the turbulent changes taking place around them. Towards the beginning of the novel, the hero, Lavretsky, comes back to re-establish himself in his real home, his "nest", after years of fruitless strivings away from his roots. We are given a long "pre-history" of the character: his family had used him as an experimental subject for all kinds of advanced educational theories, and so he had fled abroad to escape from them. There he had married a thoroughly vacuous and unscrupulous woman, who soon abandoned what she saw as an uncouth Russian backwoodsman for the greater attractions of the European rakes she encountered. Lavretsky returns to Russia without his wife, embittered but determined to justify his existence by hard work for the social good. He meets again the nineteen-year-old Liza, whom he had known when they were children. They fall in love and, when a false rumour of his wife's death reaches them, they decide to marry. However, they learn that his wife is still alive. Liza is profoundly religious and, believing that she has committed a grave sin in daring to love a married man, she enters a convent to atone. Some years later, Lavretsky visits the convent, although as an outsider he is not allowed to speak to the nuns. Liza passes by just a few feet away from him and, obviously aware of his presence, simply drops her head and clasps her rosary beads tightly to her.

However, Lavretsky, in the epilogue to the novel, seems to have achieved some measure of contentment: he has become a good landowner, and has worked very hard at improving the lot of his peasants. Therefore, he has done something positive with his life, and has to a certain extent re-established contact with his roots and ensconced himself within his Russian family "nest".

The novel was extremely popular in Russia, because it showed the country's traditional values in a positive light. This was acceptable for all sections of Russian society, both the reactionary classes and the progressives who desired political change but believed that the fount of all wisdom was to be found in indigenous rural culture.

On the Eve

The genesis of Turgenev's next novel *On the Eve* (1860) – if we are to believe Turgenev – is very peculiar. While under house arrest at Spasskoye in 1852–53, he was visited by a young local landowner, Vasily Karatayev, an army officer who was shortly due to go abroad with his regiment. Just before he departed, he gave Turgenev a story he had written, based on his own experiences as a student in Moscow, when he'd had an affair with a girl who then left him for a Bulgarian patriot. Karatayev felt he had neither the time nor the talent to work this tale up into a decent artistic work, and asked Turgenev to do so. Turgenev later claimed that Karatayev had died in the Crimean War of 1854–56, and so some years later he had devoted himself to reworking the officer's original sketch.

In the story, Yelena Stakhova, a Russian girl, falls in love with a Bulgarian patriot, Dmitry Insarov, who is an exile in Russia striving to free his country from its Turkish overlords. He and Yelena marry, and leave for Bulgaria together. However, on the way there, he falls seriously ill and dies in Venice. She decides to take on his struggle for Bulgarian freedom and continues to Bulgaria, where she becomes a nurse. After a few letters home, she is never heard of again. There is a brief meditation at the end of the novel on the death of such young, idealistic people. However much Turgenev admired them, he also, with his usual objectivity, seems to have found them slightly naive and perhaps even rather unpleasantly fanatical.

When the work appeared in the *Russian Herald*, the twenty-three-year-old radical critic Nikolai Dobrolyubov issued a long review which, though very warm in praise of the novel's style and Turgenev's sympathy for his characters, took issue with his objectivity and impersonality. He declared that this kind of standpoint was now obsolete and irrelevant, and that writers should take an explicit position as to the necessity of improving the conditions of life around them.

Fathers and Children

Sometimes erroneously translated as *Fathers and Sons*, *Fathers and Children* (1862) is generally considered to be Turgenev's masterpiece. In this novel he attempts to portray the kind of Russian "new man" who has energy and drive, and is actively striving to alter Russian society.

In a letter to an acquaintance, Countess Lambert, Turgenev claimed that he had the first idea of the novel while walking along the beach at Ventnor on the Isle of Wight, but in a later article, 'Concerning *Fathers and Children*', he tells his readers that he thought of it while swimming in the sea off the same town.

Between the writing of *On the Eve* and *Fathers and Children* a vast social change had taken place in Russia: the serfs had at last, in March 1861, been emancipated from their owners. Perhaps buoyed up by this positive trend in Russian social life, Turgenev sat down to write a novel with a central character, Yevgeny Bazarov, who is an idealistic young doctor describing himself as a "nihilist" – a word which, as we have seen before, in this context has a positive connotation, signifying someone who subjects every commonly held viewpoint or belief to profound rational analysis.

The story begins in May 1859. Arkady, a young university student who has just graduated, brings back to his father's estate a university friend, Yevgeny Bazarov, who is a newly qualified doctor and the only son of a family living on a small country estate. Bazarov represents the new young, idealistic, scientific mentality in Russian society. While there, Yevgeny becomes involved in violent arguments both with Arkady's father, who is a well-meaning liberal, and particularly with his uncle who, for all his Western ways, is an inveterate reactionary.

Love interest is provided by the appearance of Anna Odintsova, described as a frivolous woman who spends most of her time reading silly French novels. Bazarov has always scoffed at love as being irrational, but despite that he becomes infatuated with her and has to accept that not everything can be explained scientifically.

After a couple of weeks, Bazarov finally goes back home to his parents. His father is a retired doctor who still occasionally goes out to tend the local peasantry free of charge. Bazarov accompanies his father on some of these missions, and one day, while carrying out an autopsy on a typhus victim without any disinfectant, he accidentally cuts himself and becomes infected with the disease, soon falling ill and dying. His heartbroken parents are depicted as visiting his grave right into their old age, while beautiful but indifferent nature looks on.

The story was met with total incomprehension across the political spectrum, with radical reviewers calling Bazarov a malicious caricature of Dobrolyubov, while the conservative press accused him of prostrating himself to the radicals and grovelling at their feet.

Smoke

Although the idea for his next novel, *Smoke*, may have occurred to Turgenev as early as 1862, shortly after the publication of *Fathers and Children*, he took more than five years to write it, and it was not published until March 1867. He began drafting *Smoke* in Baden-Baden in November 1864, and most of the story takes place there, over less than a fortnight in August 1862, among the large community of wealthy Russians living in the town. The central character, the thirty-year-old Grigory Litvinov, after completing his university education in Western Europe, is awaiting the arrival of his fiancée Tatyana, who is also holidaying in Western Europe, so that they can return to Russia together. However, in Baden-Baden he meets Irena, a woman he had known and been infatuated with some ten years before, now married to another man. Their love affair is rekindled. He breaks off his engagement to Tatyana and begs Irena to run off with him, but she does not have the courage to do so. Litvinov returns to Russia desolate and alone. After several years, he becomes a successful farmer on his estate, meets Tatyana again. She forgives him and they marry.

The title derives from the frequent appearance in the novel of smoke (such as when Litvinov is on the train back to Russia and the smoke from the steam engine is billowing around both sides of his carriage, making the surroundings almost invisible) as a symbol of the confusion and futility of life.

Most of the critics deplored the novel, both for its immorality – a married woman falling in love with an old flame – and for its negative – indeed, almost contemptuous – portrait of the typical Russians who lived abroad.

Virgin Soil

The background of *Virgin Soil* (1877) is the great movement of young idealistic students, most of them from the educated and moneyed classes, who from the late 1860s through to the early 1870s "went to the people". Living among the peasantry and urban working classes, they shared their work and living conditions – and, of course, tried to imbue them with modern democratic ideals. Especially among the reactionary country people these youths were met with anything from amusement to contempt, and in many cases were actually handed over to the police by them as troublemakers, leading to large-scale trials, with many of the radicals being exiled to Siberia and other remote areas of the Russian Empire.

The story, the most complex and ambitious that Turgenev ever attempted, presents many minor characters and subsidiary plots. Mashurina is a follower of the fanatical and charismatic Vasily Nikolayevich. However, not all his adherents are uncritical of him – for example Nezhdanov, with whom Mashurina is in love, who is too objective and sceptical to follow anybody unquestioningly. The illegitimate and impecunious son of a nobleman, he has to earn his living by tutoring the children of wealthy reactionary members of the aristocracy and high government bureaucrats. Nezhdanov, who is in love with Maryanna, another naive radical, proves to be a "superfluous man" – unsure both of his revolutionary ideals and of his love for Maryanna. He is, more than anything else, an aristocrat who longs to be a peasant, and a poet and dreamer, not a political activist.

Nezhdanov and Maryanna run off together, and are given protection by Solomin, a rural factory manager who, although not a revolutionary, is sympathetic to those who want change. He is the novel's real hero, a hard-working modern man: he has studied science and maths, and lived and worked in Britain. He – like Turgenev – believes in slow and patient change. Nezhdanov, trying to become one of the local peasantry, simply succeeds in drinking himself into stupor in the local pubs and having to be carried back home. Solomin persuades Maryanna that she can be far more useful to the common people, not by trying to spread revolutionary ideals, but by becoming a nurse or teacher to the local children. Humiliated as a result of his failure to communicate with the local working people, and even more depressed when he realizes that he and Maryanna are drifting apart, Nezhdanov writes to Maryanna and Solomin telling them to marry each other, then he shoots himself. Maryanna and Solomin plan to get married and, although we are never told what happens in the end, they presumably devote themselves to the improvement of society in the ways advocated by Solomin. As mentioned before, barely one month after *Virgin Soil* had been published, as Turgenev was being criticized in Russia as out of touch with the present reality of the country, fifty-two young people were arrested – of whom eighteen were women.

Select Bibliography

Biographies:
Magarshack, David, *Turgenev: A Life* (London: Faber and Faber, 1954)
Pritchett, Victor, *The Gentle Barbarian: The Life and Work of Turgenev* (London: Chatto and Windus, 1977)
Schapiro, Leonard, *Turgenev: His Life and Times* (Oxford: OUP, 1978)
Troyat, Henri, *Turgenev*, tr. Nancy Amphoux (London: W.H. Allen, 1989)
Yarmolinsky, Avrahm, *Turgenev: The Man, His Art and His Age* (New York, NY: Orion Press, 1959)

Additional Recommended Background Material:
Andrew, Joe, Offord, Derek and Reid, Robert, eds., *Turgenev and Russian Culture* (Amsterdam and New York, NY: Rodopi, 2008)
Beaumont, Barbara, tr. and ed., *Flaubert and Turgenev: A Friendship in Letters* (London: Athlone Press, 1985)
Costlow, Jane, *Worlds within Worlds: The Novels of Ivan Turgenev* (Princeton, NJ: Princeton University Press, 1990)
Freeborn, Richard, *Turgenev – the Novelist's Novelist: A Study* (Oxford: Oxford University Press, 1963)
Lowe, David, tr., *Turgenev: Letters* (Ann Arbor, MI: Ardis, 1983)
Lowe, David A., ed., *Critical Essays on Ivan Turgenev*, (Boston, MA: G.K. Hall and Co., 1989)
Moser, Charles A., *Ivan Turgenev* (New York, NY, and London: Columbia University Press, 1972)
Waddington, Patrick, *Turgenev and England* (London: Macmillan, 1980)
Woodward, James, *Turgenev's* Fathers and Sons (London: Bristol Classical Press, 1996)

On the Web:
eis.bris.ac.uk/~rurap/novelsof.htm